PORTRAIT OF US

fLiRT

Read the entire Flirt series!

PORTRAIT OF US

A. DESTINY AND RHONDA HELMS

SIMON PULSE

NEW YORK   LONDON   TORONTO   SYDNEY   NEW DELHI

SIMON PULSE

An imprint of Simon & Schuster Children's Publishing Division

1230 Avenue of the Americas, New York, NY 10020

This Simon Pulse edition August 2015

Text copyright © 2014 by Simon & Schuster, Inc.

Cover photograph copyright © 2015 by Robert Daly/Getty Images

All rights reserved, including the right of reproduction in whole or in part in any form.

SIMON PULSE and colophon are registered trademarks of Simon & Schuster, Inc.

For information about special discounts for bulk purchases, please contact Simon & Schuster Special Sales at 1-866-506-1949 or business@simonandschuster.com.

The Simon & Schuster Speakers Bureau can bring authors to your live event. For more information or to book an event contact the Simon & Schuster Speakers Bureau at 1-866-248-3049 or visit our website at www.simonspeakers.com.

Designed by Regina Flath

The text of this book was set in Adobe Caslon Pro.

Manufactured in the United States of America

10 9 8 7 6 5 4 3 2 1

Library of Congress Control Number 2014931412

ISBN 978-1-4814-5190-1 (pbk)

ISBN 978-1-4814-0519-5 (eBook)

PORTRAIT OF US

Chapter ☮ One

I couldn't quite get the color of her hair right.

I stepped back from my oil canvas and tried to eye the painting with a fresh, unbiased perspective. I'd already blocked in the background colors for my portrait, soft hues of green and blue that complemented the model's flowing peach dress.

Maiko sat facing us, her long hair a rich brown-black that draped across her shoulder like a dark river. Her perfect skin was creamy, pale with blushing undertones, and her small hands rested on her lap. She was a great model, motionless but somehow still filled with life, drawing our attention to her naturally.

I'd totally captured the gentle emotion on her face, the relaxed lines of her body. But I wasn't pleased with the tones I'd mixed for her hair. They didn't feel . . . warm enough, somehow. What was I doing wrong? A bubble of frustration welled in me.

"Coming along great, Corinne," Teni Achebe, the local artist-in-residence who ran our summer workshop, said as she slipped behind me. She studied my painting, head tilted, taking in everything.

I suddenly felt like she could see every flaw, and I fought the urge to cover the whole thing with my hands. "I don't know what I'm messing up about her hair," I finally confessed, my face flushed hot. I rubbed the back of my neck with my clean hand. "It's falling flat for me."

"Hmm. Take a close look at the shades in her hair," she instructed, pointing me toward Maiko, who sat serenely, staring off into space. "You have the browns and blacks, but do you see a hint of red, too? That's the warm tone your painting is missing."

Wow. Now that she pointed it out, I could see a touch of red where the soft light hit the crown of her hair. How had I missed that?

"Thank you," I said, pouring appreciation into my voice.

"Just a thin layer over what you've already painted. Make it light, almost transparent, and I think you'll see that warmth you desire pop right out." She smiled at me, her dark brown eyes crinkling in the corners.

Teni, a tall slender African woman, was in her forties, with only a few hints of gray threading through her many braids. She wore gold bangle bracelets, her dress bearing an abstract batik pattern in bright red, green, and purple. Teni had moved to Ohio from Nigeria as a young girl and had worked in retail for a number of years, but her art had exploded a few years ago when she'd been featured in a New York gallery opening. Her five paintings had sold within a few hours for jaw-dropping prices, and things had gone uphill for her ever since.

Last year Teni had opened a summer residency program for local Cleveland area high schoolers, grades ten through twelve, who were interested in seriously studying art under her tutelage. I'd spent much of my tenth grade year waiting in nervous antici-pation to see if I'd made the list. When I'd finally gotten the call from her right before the school year ended, I'd squealed for about an hour.

"Keep up the good work," Teni said with a smile as she moved on to the guy at the easel beside me. He looked up at her in des-perate hope as she leaned closer and started whispering tips on how to make the face more realistic.

I turned my attention back to my painting, created the thin red wash, and layered it over her hair. It was a subtle touch, but it made all the difference. I couldn't fight the smile that crept over my face. After a few more minutes of fussing with minor details, I paused and put my brush down. I needed a small brain break.

Curiosity finally overtook me, and I scanned the rest of the room to see how everyone else's projects were going. Being in the middle of the room, I was able to check out a number of other students' artwork. Our studio was roomy but not too big, with a dozen stations spread throughout.

Sunlight poured in from rows of large windows, sending rays across our art—Teni had insisted from day one that the key to amazing art was good lighting, no matter what your media was. So she kept all the blinds open every class. Fortunately, she also kept the air-conditioning kicked on to prevent the room from getting overly hot.

There were a couple of people scattered around who were doing classical oil paintings like me. I saw a guy working with watercolor as he painted Maiko's hair. One of the girls near the front was doing her piece entirely in pen; she painstakingly drew hatch marks for shading and created 3-D tones that awed me.

I had to admit—her artwork looked fabulous from where I was standing. She'd captured Maiko's almond-shaped eyes and high cheekbones, the twinkle of life in her irises, despite it all being black and grayscale. Maybe I needed to work on deepening my darker tones.

My attention then caught on the tall guy standing beside her, wearing long black shorts and a plain white T-shirt. His brown hair was tousled, as if he'd run his hands through it multiple times. Matthew Bonder—he attended my school and had also just finished his sophomore year, a basketball player who generally hung out with a bunch of jocks. I bit back an irritated sigh and looked at his . . . painting, I guess you could call it. It was very postmodern, with strokes of abstract black lines I supposed were meant to represent the model's form. I could hardly find a face on the page.

I knew it was kind of snobby to think so, but that just wasn't real art for me. I liked actually being able to discern features, to see the meticulous effort of re-creating life around us. Abstract stuff was confusing—it felt like the artist was trying to pass off something that had taken all of five minutes to create.

How had he even gotten into this class?

I think I'd talked to Matthew a total of five seconds our entire freshman and sophomore years. Needless to say, we ran in different circles. I was captain of the mathlete team, president of our school's French club. My friends and I didn't really hang at any sporting events except for the occasional football game. It took a lot of academic focus to maintain my 4.0 GPA, but I did it.

Matthew, on the other hand, had sat in the back row of our few shared classes, barely speaking a word. Who even knew what grades he was making? From what I could tell, he funneled all of his discernible attention into sports—basketball, baseball, golf. I'd never seen him show any interest in art, so it had floored me when I'd walked in the door a couple of weeks ago and there he was.

As if he could sense my thoughts, Matthew looked over his shoulder and locked eyes with me. My face burned from getting caught staring at him and his work, and I swallowed. He simply raised an eyebrow and gave the smallest shadow of a smile, his dark blue eyes sparkling just a touch.

I tore my gaze away and fixed my eyes firmly back on my own painting. Crud. That was awkward.

The rest of the class session went pretty fast. I worked on adding small details to my painting—her fingernails, the thin brows above her eyes, the lace on the bottom of her dress. I was almost done with my piece, which was good; we'd been working on this particular project, our first as a group, for a solid couple of weeks now.

What would be our next big class project? I was excited to move on and do something new and challenging.

"Wow. I'm so proud of your progress," Teni said as she moved to the front of the room. Her dress swirled around her slender legs, and she propped a hand on Maiko's shoulder, giving her a grateful smile. "Before class ends for the day, I wanted to discuss an opportunity I think a few of you might be interested in."

Opportunity? I found myself perking up. I put down my paintbrush and gave her my full attention.

"Every year there's a nationwide art competition, with artists like myself sponsoring promising high school students to enter. It's hard work—you *really* have to push yourself beyond what you think you're capable of, because you're competing with the entire United States."

There was a collective "ooh" from the class. My stomach tightened in anticipation. I knew right then that whatever it was, I wanted in. Nothing excited me more than a good challenge, and growing in my art craft would be a bonus.

"This year's competition is . . ." She paused, gave a smile. "Well, it's unique. But I have a feeling my students will rise to the occasion. The prize is five thousand dollars, plus an all-expense-paid trip for you and your family to New York City to see your artwork on display in a real gallery at a notable exhibition. Plus, that artwork will be featured in a full-page spread in a national magazine—and I can't say which one yet, because that's still in the works and nothing is finalized. But you've all heard of it, I'm sure." She winked.

I was fairly certain my heart stopped beating for a moment. All the blood rushed to my ears, and when my pulse finally kick-started again, it roared in my head.

Wow. That was a huge prize.

"Miss Achebe," the line-drawing girl in the front said, raising her hand, "when does the competition take place? And how do we enter?"

"I'm getting right to that, Natalia," she said with a smile. She turned her attention to all of us. "I spent these first couple of weeks here evaluating your art, getting a sense of who you all are. What skills you have and how you need to grow. I firmly believe any of you would do a fantastic job in the competition. But the timeline is very short." Her face turned serious. "I need you to present to me your best work of art, the one that most represents your style and technique, by Friday after class. The judging for the competition will take place just over a month from now."

There were a couple of dismayed gasps.

Teni held up her hands. "Look, I know that is a very short turnaround, but if you want it badly enough, you can do it. You have a few days to either find a piece in your *oeuvre* or create something new. And it can't be the piece you used to get into this workshop," she added with a regretful smile. "I've already seen that one. Push yourselves to dig deep and wow me. I'm only going to sponsor the best, because it's a time and money investment for me. But I know it'll be worth it."

I scrabbled through my memory to see if I had anything in my room, in my portfolio that might work. There were a few pictures I'd drawn—but of course, my best piece I'd already used to get into this class.

No, I would just have to create something new. But what?

"If you have any questions for me, I'm available to talk more after class. For now, go ahead and use the remaining time to finish your work for the day and clean up your stations."

The guy beside me muttered, "No way I'd be ready in time. I barely got into this class to begin with. Are you gonna enter?"

I nodded. "Not sure what I'm going to paint though. I'm not quite satisfied with the stuff I already have."

He gave me a big grin, picking up his brush—loaded with acrylic paint—and rinsing it. He was gawky, with a shock of black hair and thick brows, and wore trendy horn-rimmed glasses. His smile was friendly. "Well, good luck. I think you'll do a great job." He nodded toward my painting. "That looks amazing. Just like her."

"Thanks." With dismay, I realized I'd never introduced myself to him. "I'm Corrine, by the way."

"Henry." He stuck out a hand and shook mine. "I go to Berea High School—I'm going to be a senior. You?"

"I'm here in Lakewood," I said. "I'll be a junior." Wow, it still felt great to say that.

"Nice to finally 'meet' you." He finished rinsing his brushes in his small cup and took his palette to the washing station in the corner, where there were several big sinks.

I used turpentine to clean the oil paint off my brushes, straightened my station, and gingerly stepped around my painting, not wanting to disturb the still-wet paint. I ran smack into a tall, lean chest. "Oh, sorry," I said, holding up a hand and stepping back.

Matthew peered down at me, one side of his mouth upturned. "No, I'm sorry. I was just barreling right through here."

I gave a tight smile and moved past him to toss my paper towels. Then I told Teni I'd see her on Wednesday, grabbed my backpack, and headed out the door, stepping into the hot sunshine. June in Cleveland could be surprisingly humid, and we were in a particularly dry spell right now.

I was extra fortunate that the art workshop was only a mile away from my house, so I hoofed it down the sidewalk blocks here in Lakewood, past small consignment shops and mom-and-pop diners. I loved the vibe of this neighborhood—the eclectic mix of people, the art galleries and jewelry stores scattered around. The sun beat down on the back of my neck, and sweat dribbled along my collar, sliding down my spine. Wow, it was a warm one today.

I turned my focus back to the issue at hand. What art project was I going to do? The pressure wrapped itself around my chest, squeezing my lungs. I was excited—and petrified. Maybe Grandpa could give me some ideas. Yeah, I wasn't going to be helping at the bakery until Saturday, but maybe I could give him a call.

Grandpa was a bit of an artist himself, though his focus was on food. He'd opened the bakery about thirty years ago, and it had grown into a staple in our neighborhood. His cakes were to die for—rich, decadent, with decorations that blew my mind. As much as I loved painting and drawing, somehow I could never get the hang of using those little frosting bags. My work always turned out too lumpy.

He would take the bag from me with a laugh and fix the mistakes, making them look like they were intentional. I was in awe of his skills.

I let my gaze wander around the neighborhood, watched kids playing on the street, drawing with hot-pink chalk and giggling. One little girl had fat braids on both sides of her head. Her skin tone matched mine, a dark brown with golden undertones. Reminded me of when I was a kid, sitting with my younger brother at the park, both of us wearing brightly colored outfits and posing for Mom's camera.

I stopped in place. That would be fun—maybe I could paint a picture from a photograph of when I was younger. It would certainly challenge me. And my mom had hundreds of pictures in her albums. Surely I could find one that would work. I could paint it in acrylics or watercolor so it would dry in time. Not as challenging as oil painting, but either medium still gave me the ability to make something worthwhile.

My heart fluttered. This was going to happen. A chance for me to do something big. Yes, I'd had a lot of accomplishments in my life, things I was proud of. Academic achievements that I'd worked hard for. But nothing would compare to winning a nationwide art contest.

Being in a gallery. In New York City.

The stakes were high, and from looking at the artwork of several of the fellow artists in my room, the competition was stiff. But I had to make this work. I'd spend all my free time working on this piece.

I wasn't going to fail. I would put my heart and soul into it, and pray, pray, pray that it was good enough for me to qualify.

Chapter ☙ Two

"Mom, can you please pass the green beans?" I reached a hand out for the bowl.

She gave me a good-natured grin and handed them to me. "I swear, you're the only one in this house who always appreciates my cooking."

I didn't know what she did to the green beans, other than adding in small pieces of fresh bacon, but they were to die for. My friend Ava also loved coming over for family-night dinner as much as possible because Mom would shove enough food at her to feed an army. I scooped another helping onto my plate. "Well, I'm a growing girl. I gotta keep up my energy."

My twelve-year-old brother, Charlie, rolled his eyes at me. I knew he thought I was kissing up. Mom shot him a warning glance, and he turned his attention back to his half-eaten pork chop.

"So how was your art class today?" Dad asked me. He took the bowl and put it back in the middle of the table, then scooped a forkful of mashed potatoes. His thick black hair was cropped close to his head, and his dark eyes twinkled in the dining room light. "You're still keeping up on your math work, right? I just want to make sure this isn't going to interfere with academics."

Despite the fact that it was summer, my dad had me working from a twelfth-grade math book to make sure I didn't lose my place as mathlete captain when I started junior year in the fall. Academics came first, everything else second. "Every night, Dad. And art class went well today. I'm almost done with my oil painting of the model."

"Good girl." He gave me an approving nod.

I started to tell him about the competition, but I was interrupted when Charlie groaned. "Doesn't anyone care what *I* did today?"

"And what did you do, honey?" my mom asked him. Her cocoa skin glowed especially warm on her cheeks today, and she shoved her three-quarter sleeves up her forearms; she must have eaten her lunch outside, a rare treat for her.

Mom worked as an investment specialist at a local bank, a job that was pretty demanding of her during the weekday. Though she usually got up and left early in the morning, it was her firm rule that everyone would be home in time for dinner at least one night a week. Pretty much the only time we all sat down to talk.

Dad worked at home most days. His job in graphic design

meant he could work flexible hours, in his home office. So we saw him a lot more than we did Mom.

Charlie launched into a five-minute, rapid-fire description of how he and his best friend, thirteen-year-old Maxine, had worked on a solar-powered car this morning and then discussed their class schedule for the fall. Both were entering eighth grade and talked about it nonstop. To be honest, I was kinda getting tired of hearing about it over and over again. "So Maxine and I aren't in any classes together for eighth grade, but we should still be able to see each other for lunch. Anyway, this week we're going to see if we can make our car go faster. I think the wood we used isn't quite right. Maybe some balsa might be lighter and more flexible. Can you take us to the store tomorrow, Dad?"

Mom and Dad exchanged a small, knowing look. Over the last couple of weeks it seemed everyone but Charlie had noticed that Maxine had a small crush on him. It was painfully awkward yet so cute, like she'd suddenly realized my brother was a boy. And she liked boys. Specifically him.

Poor Charlie was still clueless though. No doubt it would be highly entertaining when he started to notice how pretty Maxine was. Even more entertaining when he realized *other* guys found Maxine attractive. Then he'd be forced to actually do something about it.

"Sure, we'll make something work," Dad said.

I cleared my throat, wanting to get their attention before my brother went on another rambling spiel. "Teni, the artist in residence, told our class something interesting today." I briefly explained the contest and the prizes.

"That sounds challenging and fun. But are you sure you have time for this?" Mom asked, a deep line in her brow. "It sounds like it'll be intensive. Plus, with you working at Grandpa's bakery . . . You're already so busy."

A small swell of frustration pinched my stomach. I was juggling everything I needed to just fine. Why were they continually thinking I couldn't accomplish it all? I tried to keep my irritation out of my voice, not wanting to tick them off and risk them saying I couldn't enter. "I've got it all handled," I promised. "Our entry project is not due until Friday, so I have time. I'll be starting it tonight. After my math problems," I added, looking at my dad.

He nodded. "Okay. Just . . . don't overload yourself. There's not a lot of time left until school starts. I don't want you getting behind."

The hard part was, I knew they meant well. They wanted me to succeed at school, at life. Time and time again they had told me that if I was going to do something, I needed to give it 100 percent. Otherwise, why waste my time?

But my gut told me this wasn't a waste. It would be a coup of an accomplishment. Something I could be genuinely proud of. Yes, I was strong in academics, but how was I advancing myself in the arts? What better opportunity could I get to make myself more well-rounded?

"If I think I'll get overwhelmed, I'll back out," I told them, knowing it wasn't going to happen but wanting to give them a little peace of mind.

They both nodded, and we all finished dinner in relative silence. Charlie devoured his food first and jumped right out of his seat when Mom gave him the nod to excuse him from the table. He grabbed his plate, silverware, and cup and practically ran into the kitchen to rinse them. I followed closely behind, then escaped to the sanctuary of my bedroom.

When I closed the door behind me, I gave a relieved sigh and dropped back against the door. My room truly was the one place I could most relax. The walls were painted green, with a purple accent wall. I had artistic posters up that I'd hung to inspire my creativity, images by all the classic painters. A massive print of *Girl with a Pearl Earring* by Vermeer was right above my bed, a recent favorite I'd acquired.

Simply beautiful. I breathed in, shook out the slight tension in my shoulders that had lingered from the dinner conversation, and headed to my bed. Earlier today I'd found the perfect picture, one my mom had taken of me and Charlie when I was around seven and he was just four. We were at the beach, and the sunlight made our skin luminous, our eyes bright and wide. Somehow she'd captured a childlike innocence on our faces. A moment of sheer happiness.

I remembered that day, how fun it had been. A rare occasion when my mom called off work, gathered me, Charlie, and my dad in the car, and drove us to the lake for an impromptu day of fun. Charlie and I had been sitting at home bored, since it was a teacher in-service day.

We'd stayed at the lake for hours, laughing and splashing, eating ice cream and running through the sand.

I smiled, stroking a finger over my dad's smiling face in the background. Wow, it had been so long since then. I couldn't remember the last family vacation we'd gone on. I exhaled heavily and pushed that out of my head. Life was like that. My mom was important at the bank, my dad climbing the ladder of success with his company. Charlie and I were striving to do the same at school.

I grabbed my easel and set up my station, then remembered I'd promised I would work on math first. But my head was already in the art zone; I was staring at the blank canvas and envisioning what I would sketch to rough out my picture.

Maybe I could do math later. And he'd never know.

A guilty thrill swept through me. I grabbed my pencils and started sketching, blocking in where my brother and I were, the direction of our bodies and faces. Pausing and erasing with the kneaded eraser, fixing, tweaking the perspectives. This was one of the most important parts. If the outline wasn't right, the rest wouldn't be right either.

Now was the time to make it perfect.

It took me a good hour, but I finally got the dimensions and rough outline of my image. I swallowed, excited as I stared at it. In my mind I could see the picture coming together perfectly.

I hoped against hope it would be good enough.

There was a small knock on my door. I jerked in surprise and laughed at myself, opening the door. My best friend, Ava, stood on the other side, smiling up at me. She was a tiny person, several inches shorter than my five foot four and probably weighed ninety pounds soaking wet. Her blond hair was trimmed in a sassy chin-length bob, and she had on a cute light-blue summer dress with a pair of tan sandals.

"Hey!" she said, reaching out to hug me. Ava was a hugger, always had been. Took me a bit to get used to it when we were kids, but now I couldn't imagine our relationship being anything else. "Am I interrupting? Your mom said I could come up. She figured you'd be done with math by now." Ava made a face. Unlike most of my friends at school, she was a full-fledged artistic person and made no bones about hating math.

"Oh, uh, I haven't started it yet," I stammered.

"What?" She pressed a slender hand to my brow. "Are you sick?"

I rolled my eyes. "Hardy-har. No, I'm working on an art project."

"How's that going?" Ava bounded into my room, and I closed the door behind her. She stopped when she looked at my sketch with the original picture pinned on the corner of the easel. "Oh, that is going to be amazing," she said on a long exhale. "I love this picture of you guys. You look so cute."

"Thanks." I filled her in on the details of the contest. "So I'm trying to hurry and get it done before then, because I have to enter."

She groaned and smoothed a hand over her hair, her green eyes slanted in disappointment. "I *knew* I should have joined the workshop. That sounds like so much fun. New York City." Ava had toyed with the idea but ultimately decided she didn't want to. While she was artistic, she preferred focusing on photography and letting the muse lead her. Plus, it was a time commitment she hadn't been sure she wanted to commit to. "Who else do you think is going to try to enter?"

I shrugged, plopping down onto the bed beside her and tucking a soft white pillow across my lap. "I have no idea. There are some great artists in there."

"Anyone from our school in your class?"

I tilted my head. "Um, there's Becca Venn from English last year. Remember her? The one who always had ink all over her hands?" She was constantly drawing while in class, not even caring about trying to hide it. "And Matthew Bonder, the basketball jock," I added.

Her eyes widened, and she fanned herself. "Matthew is in there with you? How do you even concentrate long enough to get anything done?"

"Please. He isn't that attractive." Okay, that was a bit of a lie. His nose had a slight bump in it, but rather than detract from his masculine features, it gave him a bit of character. He had a classic profile, a strong jaw, piercing eyes.

Her eyebrow rose. "Uh-huh."

"Whatever," I said, brushing her off.

"What if the teacher sponsors his project?"

I thinned my lips. "Doubt it. He'll probably draw something five minutes before Friday's class and hand it in. If he even enters, that is. He puts no effort into his work, just a bunch of weird scribbles and lines."

She frowned. "Hey, now. Just because you don't get modern art doesn't mean it doesn't have value. The art world is big enough to appeal to everyone, regardless of personal taste."

"Sorry, sorry," I said, hands held up in a truce gesture. She was right. I was all classical, but Ava loved anything and everything. I didn't want to offend my best friend. "That was rude of me." Obviously Teni had seen something in his art.

"Okay, thanks." She smiled again and smoothed the front of her dress. The air-conditioning kicked on and ruffled her hem as her legs dangled over the side of my bed. "Well, I hope it works out for you. And if you get bored, draw some pictures of him for me." She waggled her eyebrows.

I snorted a laugh. "Yeah, sure, because that's super subtle. He'll never notice that at all."

Ava stood. "I won't keep you from your art. I just wanted to say hi. We're going to visit my aunt in Kentucky over the weekend, so let's plan to hang out next week sometime? You can tell me more about your class and how unattractive you think Matthew is." She crooked her mouth in a knowing grin.

"Okay," I said with a groan. "He's . . . attractive. I'll give you that." I remembered the way his blue eyes had fixed on me, and my face flushed all over again. "But he's my competition. Besides, he and I have nothing in common." I didn't care about sports at all. I didn't like his art style. What would he and I even talk about? If the chance ever arose to talk, that was. Um, not that it would, because I was going to stay focused.

"Uh-huh. Maybe if you sat down and talked to him, you'd find out you have more in common than you think. Like, maybe he enjoys chick flicks and Chinese takeout too." She giggled.

I shoved her lightly. "Sure. Maybe he and I can discuss the artistic values of our school logo."

Ava gave me a quick hug. "Text me a picture when you're done," she said. "I'm eager to see how this one turns out."

When she left, I turned back to my drawing. A good start for today. Tomorrow I'd block in the base colors and make the image come to life. And pray that my technique was strong enough to make my painting stand out among the crowd.

Chapter ● Three

The small old woman stared hard at the croissants. She tapped her wrinkled lips with a pudgy hand. "I can't decide if I want three or four," she mused.

I smiled and dusted my flour-coated hands on my jeans. "Take your time, Miss Figler. I'm right over here if you need anything." I stepped a few feet to the left and kneaded the pizza dough a little more, getting it to just the right texture.

"Corinne?" she asked. "I think I'll have four. And a couple of your grandfather's scones. They're the best I've had since I visited England."

"Grandpa loved London," I told her. "I think he studied under a baker while he was there." I prepared her order and boxed them, then rang her up. Then I divided the pizza dough into separate bags and popped them in the freezer.

Saturday mornings were either super slow or super busy. Right now we were having a slow stretch. But it gave me time to get caught up on packaging call-in orders, make more dough, and clean up my station.

The only downside was, I wasn't quite distracted enough to keep my mind off my art project. In yesterday's class, I'd turned in my entry. I'd stayed up late every night this week working on getting it just perfect. Long after my family had turned in, I'd hovered around my easel, washing layer after layer of watercolor over the image.

When I'd put the last touches on it on Thursday night, I'd collapsed in exhaustion in bed and nearly overslept yesterday morning.

Almost every student in class had turned in a piece for the competition. My stomach had been in knots. A few students in there I'd anticipated, sure—but I hadn't expected that many people. The weekend was going to drag painfully slowly, especially if we didn't get more customers in.

My grandfather popped his head out and gave me a wink. His dark golden eyes glinted in the bakery's lights. "Everything okay out here?"

I grabbed the bleach and began scrubbing down the counters. Grandpa ran a tight ship, and he insisted on the place being clean. *A sloppy shop turns customers off,* he always preached to me.

"Things are fine," I replied. "It's a little slow but not horribly so."

Grandpa stepped out and surveyed my progress. He nodded. "Doing a good job. Keep up the hard work."

I warmed under his praise. He was a tough boss, one who pushed me to do better. If I was giving a 100 percent, he wanted a hundred and ten. But this job had taught me a lot so far. Plus, having extra money in my pocket—that I'd earned myself—was never a bad thing.

"How's things at home?" he asked as he walked to the bread shelf and straightened the loaves.

"Good. Mom asked if you wanted to come over for dinner tomorrow, by the way," I said.

His nod was short. "Can do."

Grandma had passed away a few years ago, from cancer. He'd loved her heart and soul, and though he wasn't one to show a lot of emotion, her death had broken his heart. We'd all been worried that Grandpa would pull away, so Mom had started insisting he come over for Sunday dinner from time to time. That, plus the business, had spurred Grandpa to get out of bed every morning.

Time hadn't erased all the pain, but he was gradually getting his old self back. Mom, however, hadn't backed off on having him over regularly. But it was nice having him around.

The phone rang. He shuffled back into his office, and I heard his gruff voice as he took someone's order. Not the most emotional man, but his cakes were out of this world. And his designs . . . I didn't know how he did it. He'd never gone to art school, yet somehow they were richly decorated, sheer perfection.

While I added a few more croissants to the glass case in front of our counter, the door dinged. In walked Matthew, followed by a few of his basketball-jock friends. The guys behind him were loud, shoving each other, and I fought the urge to roll my eyes.

I had to be nice to the customers, even if they were super annoying.

Or if one of them had piercing blue eyes that kept drawing my attention back.

I was glad Grandpa wasn't here to see the hot flush on my cheeks. He was pretty astute and would see it immediately. I cleared my throat. "Can I help you?"

One of Matthew's friends, a stocky Asian who I think was going to be a senior this year, pursed his lips. He strolled to the counter, dragging his fingertips along the glass. Ugh. "I want a doughnut," he said, looking back at his two buddies.

Matthew's brow furrowed, and he bore holes into his friend's face. What was that all about?

The guy cleared his throat, then glanced back at me. "Uh, please."

At least one of them had manners—and enough common sense to make the other ones behave politely. Guess I could give Matthew a point of credit for that one. I gave a nod and walked over to the doughnut section. "What would you like?"

The guy tilted his head. His black hair was spiked in the front, and he rubbed a hand absently over the top of it. "Something loaded with chocolate."

Matthew's other friend, a guy who was in science with me this year—Thomas—came to the counter too. "Hey, get two of them. You owe me for buying you a Coke yesterday."

The first guy grumbled, then nodded.

I pulled two chocolate-covered doughnuts out and made myself look at Matthew. For some stupid reason, my pulse picked up. "Anything for you?" At least my tone was steady, even if a little chilly.

He shook his head and pursed his lips. "I'm not sure yet."

I put the doughnuts in individual minibags and rang the two guys out. They clomped to the door.

"Hey, man, you coming?" Thomas asked as he shoved his shoulder to the door. The little bell rang, and a blast of warm air burst inside.

"I'll be out in a minute," Matthew replied.

The guys shrugged, then started chowing on their doughnuts as they headed outside into the warm summer heat.

Matthew took his attention off the glass case, then gave me a crooked smile. "Sorry about them. I don't think they get enough oxygen in their brains."

That made me crack a small smile. At least he felt bad for them being such meatheads. "Anything in there interest you?"

He tilted his head, and a smile widened on his face.

"Um, what?"

"You have . . ." He reached toward me, then stopped, gesturing at my cheek. "Uh, there's a little flour . . ."

Ah, crud. I spun around and scrubbed at my cheeks. When I kneaded dough, flour got everywhere. Why hadn't I thought it would be on my face, too? Awkward. I turned back and fought the wave of embarrassment. "Thanks."

Matthew leaned toward the case, careful not to touch the glass and keep his fingers on the metal rim. "So, how did your project come along? You entered, right? I thought I saw that."

I swallowed. Somehow I hadn't anticipated him asking me about art. But of course he would. "It went fine, thanks." My spine was so stiff I could snap in half if another breeze rolled in here. What was it about him that set me on edge so much? "So . . . you entered?" I made myself ask.

"I did. Took me all week to work on my piece. I stayed up really late."

I tried to envision what postmodern art he would have worked on that could take more than ten minutes. Then I shoved that snotty thought out. Ava's words about me being judgmental popped to the forefront of my brain. "I did too, actually. I did a watercolor for my entry."

"I did an ink-and-newspaper collage for mine. Kind of a mixed media. A bit of a social commentary . . ." He gave a self-conscious shrug, then cleared his throat. "Um. Anyway. Good luck. I've seen your pieces, and you're really talented."

Wow, that was really nice of him. My heart thudded in surprise at the compliment. If Ava were here, she'd be poking me in the ribs. "Thanks. I appreciate that. And good luck to you, too."

Matthew rubbed a hand over the back of his neck. His Adam's apple bobbed as he swallowed, and I couldn't tear my gaze away. As much as I hated to admit it, he really was handsome.

"I'll see you Monday, then," he said, his grin crooked as he backed away from the counter.

I tipped my head in response and watched him turn to leave. Every movement of his was effortless, from the way his legs ate up the distance between him and the door to how his arm reached out and pushed it open. A sort of ballet, full of confidence and self-assurance.

Wow, was I getting ridiculous or what? Maybe I'd breathed too much flour in this morning. I shook those thoughts out of my head and turned my attention back to cleaning. *Focus,* I ordered myself. A guy could be as cute as he wanted, but that didn't mean he thought I was cute in return. Or that I'd even want him to.

I had enough on my plate. There was no room in there for a guy.

Especially one like Matthew.

After a long weekend, where I spent far too long last night staring at the ceiling, willing myself to fall asleep, it was finally Monday. I dressed quickly and ran downstairs. I could barely keep any breakfast down, my stomach was churning so hard.

Somehow, this had become more than just a regular art competition for me. Lying in bed, thinking about *why* it was so important, I realized the answer. I wanted to prove that I could do it—to my parents, to myself. They saw me as only academic, believed that should be my sole focus, but I wanted it all. To be a true Renaissance girl.

When I arrived in the art studio right before our class started, Teni instructed all of us that for our next project, we needed to work in a medium that was outside of our comfort zone. We were allowed to focus on any subject, any medium, so long as we were pushing our boundaries.

It took me a good fifteen minutes to decide what I wanted to try. A collage would certainly do the job. Basically it was just ripping a bunch of pieces of colored paper and pasting them in a pattern, right?

I couldn't help myself. I peeked over at Matthew to see what he was doing. He had a set of oil paints at his station, mixing colors in a really odd way. Oh, well.

The good thing about the project was that it would force me to focus on something other than the upcoming art competition. Somehow I'd suspected Teni would wait until the end of class to tell us the winner. She hadn't said a word about it since we'd arrived.

I had a potted flower in front of me and a stack of colored paper that coordinated with those colors. I spent the first chunk of time roughing in the outline for my flower, so I'd know where the paper would go. After that, I ripped them in chunks of colors, gluing and ripping and gluing. Layer upon layer, slightly overlapping.

It was messy. Glue stuck to my fingers, and I wiped them frequently. But the image was starting to flesh out. I used lighter and darker shades to give more dimension. It wasn't as pristine as I could like. The edges were so rough, spilling into each other without that clean precision that came from my usual painting.

I reached for a pair of scissors and picked up another piece of paper. Maybe I could cheat a little, at least for the outline of the flower and vase.

"When you cut, you lose that human element," Teni said as she popped up right behind me. "Embrace the imperfections, Corrine."

I sighed. "It just . . . feels wrong. It doesn't look the way I want it to." I stared in frustration at the piece. It was clunky, like a child had done it. I wanted my art to be sophisticated, not amateur.

Teni rubbed my back. "Corinne, you focus so hard on exactness. Art is messy and fun. It's challenging. It speaks words to us, makes us think. Yes, there is beauty. But there is also ugliness, and that has its place. Its own voice. Don't be afraid to let yourself go." She gave me a patient smile. "You'll find it. Just keep trying."

"Thanks." I nodded. I knew she was right on some level, but I couldn't help that I still craved beauty. And this new piece of mine wasn't doing it. Maybe I should practice ripping at home so I got cleaner lines.

Then I laughed at myself. That would defeat the purpose of what she was trying to tell me. Still, as I ripped fresh chunks of paper, I took it slower, trying to clean up my edges more.

Time flew after that. I found myself getting absorbed in the piece. I wasn't crazy about it, but I had to admit, there was something therapeutic about focusing all of your attention on finding exactly the right shade and shape of paper. I'd decided to overlap my pieces more so the entire page was covered, with no white background to be seen. It also helped me add more precision to my borders.

"Class," Teni said from in front of the room. Her loud voice startled me, and I jerked a little. She had a huge smile on her face. "Thank you for your patience. I know many of you are dying to learn the results, to see who is going to be sponsored in the nationwide art competition. So clean up your stations and when you're done . . ." She paused. "I'll tell you who I chose."

Chapter ● Four

Our class had never cleaned up our stations faster than we did at that moment. I stuffed ripped papers into baggies, wiped down the counter to clean off dried spots of glue, then stood at my table. My heart was racing so fast I thought it might gallop right out of my chest. It took everything I had not to rush around and nudge the two stragglers in the back to finish faster.

"Excellent," Teni declared. She leaned against the front wall, taking us all in with her shrewd eyes. "So, I have a confession to make first—and an explanation. I misled you all by leaving out one important detail about the competition. And the reason I did so was because I wanted to ensure I wouldn't skew your art projects. I needed to see you give your all, to focus solely on your project without being worried about the missing detail."

What could she mean? My stomach flipped in anticipation.

"I'm not sure how much you know about the competition, but it varies every year. Last year's featured mixed-media projects. The year before that was nature themed. This helps to open the contest up to new artists, encouraging them to continue to grow their skills." She paused. "This year's competition will feature two artists working together on a joint project."

My jaw dropped. Around me there were a few whispers.

"Hadn't expected that," Henry mumbled from beside me, his thick black brows raised high in surprise.

"One of the students I will be sponsoring is Matthew Bonder." She clapped and gave him a hearty smile. "Congratulations, Matthew."

I saw his back stiffen, and he blinked as he eyed the people around him, who began to heartily clap him on the back and wish him luck.

My stomach fell. Wonderful. If she was looking for art like his, that bold postmodernism that made its own rules, its own style, I was out of the running. My chest deflated and I blinked back the sting in my eyes. I wasn't going to show my crushed disappointment here.

Teni held up Matthew's project. It was a slash of dark lines across newsprint, pasted haphazardly on the page. I saw words standing out in bold print, highlighted, marked up. There were images of sad women and homeless men on the street. It was stark, dark. It made me uncomfortable.

"From the beginning, I have loved that Matthew's art challenges us. It's not beautiful. Its meaning is not immediately clear, so we have to really study it, analyze it, pull it apart. This particular piece is bold and wild. I think he'll work hard to bring a fresh spark into this competition, and I'm very excited about it."

"Thank you, Teni," he said, and I could hear the buzz of adrenaline in his voice. Of course he was thrilled. He'd gotten in.

She propped his art along the counter and then faced us all again. "And the other student is . . . Corrine Walters."

My throat closed and I stared in confusion. Had I heard that right?

Henry's large hand clapped me on the shoulder. "Congrats!" he said, shoving his glasses up his nose. A few other people around me turned to me with wide smiles, clapping.

My pulse roared in my ears. I'd made it. I'd made it! But . . . I locked eyes with Matthew, whose bold gaze raked over my face. My cheeks burned impossibly hot. I was going to be working with him.

The guy whose art was confusing and completely, utterly different from my own. How could this even work?

I exhaled slowly and gave a weak smile to everyone in return.

Teni took my piece out, and my heart squeezed as I eyed it. Yeah, there were flaws in my technique—with a couple of days' space from the project, I could see that the eyes weren't as perfect as I'd want them. "As you can tell, Corinne and Matthew have very different artistic visions."

A light chuckle rippled through the room.

"But Corinne has a way of capturing the essence of a person in a way I haven't seen in a long time. Her art has an old soul. This piece mesmerized me."

I crossed my arms over my chest, fighting back the burst of pleasure that threatened to erupt on my face. She loved my art.

The validation eased some of the sting from my shock. But I was still left with loads of confusion and frustration. How did she expect us to make this work?

Teni gave me a knowing glance. "The challenge for Matthew and Corinne is impressive. Two very different artists must blend their visions together to create a piece that reflects both of them. But I see their potential. And I think they can make something that will win the competition." She propped my piece beside Matthew's—color and subject and message so very different.

There was no way this would work. Seeing our pieces side by side reinforced that for me.

Crud.

"See you all Wednesday," Teni called out, walking over to her bag as students left the studio, each giving me and Matthew words of encouragement and praise.

But I barely heard any of it.

"Teni," I said, worming my way to the front of the room.

She slung her large patchwork bag over her shoulder. "I'm sure you have a million questions, but unfortunately I have to run to an appointment. We can talk before or after class on Wednesday, okay?"

My heart trilled in nervous response to what I was going to

say. "I . . . don't think this can work." I forced myself to speak. "We're far too different. There's no way we can make something mesh that we'll both be happy with."

Frankly, I didn't want him to ruin my work with his strange style. It was fine if he did it on his own—I didn't get it, but I could accept it. The thought of us trying to blend our styles . . . Baffling. Wearisome. Far too big of a challenge.

Teni's face lost some of its smile. "I know this is going to be hard for you. But Matthew has some things he can teach you. And vice versa."

"Is there any way we can . . . reconsider this?" I asked. I couldn't hide the thin, pleading tone in my voice.

She raised one eyebrow. "It's either both of you or neither of you. Those are my terms, Corinne. Can you accept that?"

For a moment I let myself consider the option of walking away. Letting go of this competition. But I couldn't do that. I needed this, even if it meant I had to work with him.

I gave a sullen nod.

She tipped my chin with her cool fingertips. "Smile. I promise you, by the end of the summer your whole life will be different. Your world will be sparked in a way you could never have dreamed."

I forced a smile to my face and watched her walk away. A hot flush burst on my cheeks as I realized Matthew was still standing there at his station, his own smile strained. Great, he'd overheard me. Knew I didn't want to do this with him.

I swallowed. Teni seemed to believe we could create a great

piece together. I saw disaster on the horizon. But I'd chosen my path and I was going to see this through, despite the insurmountable odds. "Um," I said, then cleared my throat. "I . . ."

"It's fine," he said, and I saw the stiffness around his mouth, the tension in his limbs. He was obviously mad about what I'd said. Then another thought came to me—maybe Matthew was hesitant about being paired up with me, too. Something I hadn't considered until now. "We can talk on Wednesday with Teni and . . . come up with whatever we want to do for our project," he continued.

My nod was weak. I gave a smile I knew looked forced, grabbed my bag, and darted out of the studio. The potential thrill of winning the competition, once so alluring, now felt impossible for me. As I walked home, small beads of sweat dripping down my back from the hot June sunshine, I couldn't get the image of our two pieces, side by side, out of my mind. Stark differences that would be difficult to overcome.

And the other image in my mind was Matthew's crestfallen face, the dull light in his blue eyes as he'd stared at me. Guilt flared anew in my chest. I should have waited to make sure he wasn't around before voicing my concerns with Teni. As much as I knew we wouldn't work out, I didn't want to be rude.

It wasn't his fault she'd picked the two of us to work together.

"I don't understand this at all," I said to Ava after chewing a bite of juicy hamburger. It was late afternoon and we were in the food court at the mall, noshing on dinner from a burger joint. Voices hummed and buzzed around us, teens and parents and guys and girls laughing, talking, eating.

When I'd gotten home from art class, in a total funk and mentally distraught, I'd sent Ava a text immediately, asking her to meet with me whenever she was done babysitting her five-year-old cousin. My brain wouldn't stop churning about this whole mess.

I needed the easy clarity of her wisdom. Ava was good at helping me get through rough spots, putting myself aside to view the big picture. If I ever needed perspective, it was right now.

Ava snagged a fallen pickle slice from her plate and popped it into her mouth, closing her eyes as she chewed in slow pleasure. Today her blond hair rocked sassy, wavy curls, and she had on jean shorts and a hot-red T-shirt. "If I could eat nothing but pickles for the rest of my life, I would."

I rolled my eyes and chuckled. "I'll remember that for your next birthday."

"Okay, back to your issue," Ava said. She dabbed a napkin at her mouth with delicate finesse, then put it on the table. "Although I have to admit . . . I don't quite understand what the problem is."

"Um, what?" Had I not explained everything clearly enough? I'd rattled on for fifteen minutes, barely taking a breath the whole time. Surely that had been enough.

She lifted a finger. "One, you made it into the competition. You're being sponsored by the artist, which is what you'd hoped for. Right?"

I reluctantly nodded. "Technically yes, but—"

"Two, he's cute. I mean, super adorable. Have you actually ever *looked* at him?" She sighed and propped her chin on her hands, elbows resting on the table, eyes glazed as she stared into the distance. "Those blue eyes pierce right through you."

I fidgeted in my seat. I wasn't quite ready to admit out loud how very, very attractive Matthew was, though I had to be honest with myself—I already knew it and had for a while. Over the weekend I'd spent more time than I cared to confess considering the nuances of smile, wondering if I could capture those deep dimples in a portrait.

Embarrassing and awkward.

I swallowed. "Well, he does have classic features that some people might find handsome," I tried in an offhand, casual tone.

Ava snorted and took another big bite of her burger. She saw right through me, of course. "Uh-huh. Some people? Try everyone in our school. Do you know how many girls would kill to be in your spot? Working one on one with him for long hours, close together, getting closer and closer?"

"If it weren't for the fact that I have to, I would gladly let all those girls have him." A miserable sensation swirled in my stomach, combined with an emotion I couldn't name. Something like nervous anticipation, speckled with dread. "I already said yes, that I'd do it, but I'm freaking out a little. What can we possibly find as a subject for our piece that we'll both agree on? He likes abstract art. I loathe it. He's a jock. I'm an egghead. We're far too different."

"You should give him a chance—a *real* chance," she added. "You might find you're not as different as you think you are."

I huffed. "Yeah, who knows? Maybe we'll both end up being cocaptains on the mathlete team next year." Okay, that wasn't nice. Just because he wasn't as intellectually driven as I was didn't mean I needed to be mean-spirited. I felt bad for making that comment and suddenly wanted to change the subject to something, anything, else. "So, you said earlier you're going on vacation with your family. Where to?"

Ava brightened up, taking the bait. "Scotland! My dad's family is from there, and he's always wanted to go back to his roots. So we're gonna go for a couple of weeks and explore our heritage. I have no idea what to expect, but I've been spending hours researching it all online."

"That sounds amazing. You have to take a bunch of pictures." I smiled.

Her face grew serious, and she reached out a hand. "Hey, it'll all work out. I know you're stressed, but I'm sure he wants to win too. You guys will figure out the perfect project."

I gave a weak grin; I knew she'd see right through it, but maybe if I kept smiling it would become genuine. Fake it till I make it, right? "Maybe you're right. I wish I had your optimism."

"Well, not everyone can be as amazing as me. It took years of refinement for me to even get to this level." Her teeth sparkled with her wide smirk.

I rolled my eyes and shook my head, smothering a low chuckle.

Leave it to Ava to find a way to pull me out of my funk. "You're crazy. In a good way. Thanks—for listening to me whine and not choking me in aggravation. I know I'm stubborn, but I just . . . I want the best. I want to *be* the best and have a fair chance at this competition. I'm nervous."

"Like I'd be anywhere else right now than here with you." Ava reached over and hugged me. "So, I do believe we have more shopping to do," she declared, cramming the last of her fries into her mouth and chewing fast. "I need some clothes for Scotland, and you need . . . well, a good distraction."

We cleared our trays and walked around the mall for a while, window-shopping for the most part, though we did buy a couple of small things. I found a red wrap bracelet that went perfectly with one of my dresses, and Ava got dangly silver earrings that brushed her shoulders. We had a great time, and my mood lightened with every goofy hat or wild scarf we tried on.

I was so thankful for her.

Ava and I had been best friends since sixth grade when, as the new girl, she sat beside me on our first day of middle school. She hadn't been shy at all about introducing herself and asking my name. And when she told me she loved my margin doodles, then showed me her own, I knew we were going to be close.

I glanced over at her as she flipped through a rack of clothes, looking for her size in a dark purple off-the-shoulder top. It was going to be lonely here when she went to Scotland. I was happy for her, but kinda jealous that I wasn't going on a fun vacation like that. My parents hardly ever took time off work. At least she would have good stories to tell when she returned and maybe have fun flirting with a boy or two while there.

I pushed all thoughts of Matthew and Scotland out of my mind and focused on enjoying this moment with my best friend.

Chapter ☙ Five

I could hear my pulse racing in my ears as I stepped through the art studio doors on Wednesday morning. The cool air smacked me in the face. It was already a scorcher out, and the sun was still rising, so I was glad for the indoor reprieve. Still, air-conditioning wasn't enough to distract me from my pending fate.

Facing Matthew. Working with him.

I'd spent a little longer than normal this morning picking out today's outfit, braiding my hair and twisting it into patterns around my head. It wasn't for him—not at all. I simply wanted to present a professional front. Mom always told me the clothes made the man . . . or woman. And she was usually right about these things.

Matthew was already at his station, working on his newest

art piece. I made my way to my station and grabbed my mosaic materials to work more on my piece.

His back to me, I took a moment to look at him closely, study him with an unbiased eye the way Ava had advised me to. The soft hair that dusted the top of his neck. The length of his hands, their strong fingers—no doubt enhanced because of his focus on sports. His striking long legs, firm calves. His shoulder blades flexing beneath the plain black T-shirt.

There was a tiny freckle above his elbow on his right arm. For some stupid reason, my fingers itched to touch it. I opened the plastic bag and took out the colored scraps of paper, then spread them across the table in front of me. Right now I was going to lose myself in the moment of creating. I blanked my mind, tilting my head to study my work in progress.

The image started to come to life. The base colors I'd layered in were working surprisingly well. I found the next shade I wanted to work with, for the flower petals, and began gluing them on. It was a rich, vibrant blue, and the petals popped.

"Lovely," Teni said as she approached my piece. "I like how you're building the image from dark to light, making sure you have those rich shadows to give depth to your work. What made you decide to do the flowers in blue?"

I shrugged. Truth was, I'd been drawn to that shade. The flower vase in front of me had yellow flowers, but my fingers had just grabbed the deep blue paper pieces. "It seemed right for the piece."

She patted my back. "Keep working. When class is over, you and Matthew stay after. We'll go over the rules and work out a schedule. You'll probably need extra studio time, and I want to supervise your sessions at least once a week so I can assist if I'm needed." Teni walked over to Henry's station, and I heard them whispering softly about his work in progress, a charcoal drawing.

It took me a full ten minutes of working on the flower to realize where that shade had come from. It matched Matthew's eyes perfectly.

Boy, did my face flush. I hoped he wouldn't notice. I couldn't believe I'd done that. Well, I couldn't deny that he was attractive, that he had striking eyes. I was appreciating him with an artist's perspective. There was no crime in that, right?

Class moved along at a nice clip. I kept my attention firmly on my piece, not looking around at any particular person as I ripped and glued and ripped and glued. It wasn't perfect, but I had to admit, there was something interesting about the roughness of my piece. I felt daring, like I was pushing my boundaries.

This was the rush of creating art, that strange, stomach-dropping, nervous anticipation of trying to take the image in your head and re-create it on paper, or canvas, or whatever.

"I'm so happy about today's progress," Teni said as she slipped up the center aisle. "You're all pushing yourselves in new directions. I know it's not comfortable, but this is how we grow. Our class is almost over, so take a few more minutes and then clean up your stations."

"Hey, Corinne." A light whisper came from behind me.

I turned to see an older teen smiling at me. Her red hair curled wildly around her head, and her face and bare arms were covered in spatters of freckles. Her teeth gapped slightly. She wasn't conventionally pretty, but her face was so friendly I couldn't help but smile back. However, I couldn't remember her name, and she didn't go to my school. How did she know who I was?

Duh, Corinne, I chastised myself. Teni had said my name out loud when announcing the results on Monday. Unlike me, this girl probably paid better attention to those details.

"Hi," I whispered back.

"I just wanted to tell you I really like your piece." She nodded toward my mosaic. "I've never tried to do that before, but you're inspiring me to pick that medium for my next project."

My heart gave a strange twist. "Thank you." I stepped back to her station so I could see what she was doing.

My breath caught in my lungs. The image was already stunning, and she was still in the drawing phase. She'd sketched Teni standing near a window, light playing along the planes of her face. There was a faint hint of a wistful smile as she stared outside.

"That's beautiful," I said.

"Oh, thanks. I couldn't resist when I saw her standing there. I grabbed my phone and took a picture so I could capture the moment." She pointed down to her phone sitting on the table. The exact same image was right there.

I had to admit, I was jealous. Why hadn't she gotten picked for the competition? She clearly outshined me with talent.

"I'm Janice, by the way," she said, offering a smile.

"Where do you go to school?"

"I just graduated from Parma High School. Heading to Baldwin Wallace in the fall. I plan to major in art history."

"That sounds great." I had no idea what I was going to do in college, though my parents were already subtly nudging me on the subject. I cleared my throat, an awkward sensation lodged in my gut. After seeing her art, I felt like she'd gotten cheated.

"Are you excited about the competition?" she asked, no hint of negativity in her tone at all.

"Oh, I . . . I'm nervous," I admitted.

"Yeah, I don't do well in those kinds of situations. I don't thrive under pressure. That's why I didn't even enter."

Ah. Okay.

Before I could process it, she continued. "Plus, after seeing the works of people in here—like you, for example—I knew I wasn't ready."

I blinked. "You're kidding, right?"

She laughed, a light, tinkling sound, and began packing away her pencils in a box. "It's been my experience so far that the artists with the most talent often don't see it. Teni knew what she was doing when she picked you. I can't wait to see the piece you two create."

My gaze slid over to Matthew unbidden, and a warm flush

worked its way up my throat. Why was I letting him get to me? Why couldn't I just shut off this strange feeling I got whenever I thought of him?

"Well, I wish you guys luck," she continued. "It's going to be quite a challenge, blending your two art styles into one cohesive piece. But I have a feeling when it's done, you will knock everyone's socks off." She slung her bag over her shoulder, gave me a parting nod, then walked out the door.

I stared at her piece for another long moment. Her style was a lot closer to mine than to Matthew's—she'd taken great pains to capture true perspective, the nuances and angles of Teni's figure, the light and dark. But there was a rawness in her sketch lines that showed me she wasn't as concerned with clean edges as I was. I could see where she'd corrected her lines without erasing the old ones. She didn't have that compulsion for perfection.

And yet, her piece came to life and would only continue to grow in beauty as she finished it. Interesting.

I filed that nugget away and headed to the front of the room, where Teni perched against a table along the wall. Matthew came up right behind me, and I swear I could feel the warmth pouring from his body into mine. I took a small step forward to get out of that mode of hyperawareness. I needed to focus, not think about him like that.

Like a guy I found attractive.

"Thank you both for agreeing to work together," Teni started. She pointed to a stack of magazines and newspapers. "What I want from you two today is twofold: First, get to know each other. You're both very different people, and yet I think you have more in common than you realize."

Why did people keep saying that? And it was so untrue. He and I were nothing alike. I stopped the sarcastic huff that wanted to come out. I heard a small chuckle behind me and peeked at him over my shoulder. His eyes were looking down at mine, and he seemed like he was laughing.

At me? My spine stiffened.

Teni didn't seem to notice the thickening tension between us. "And second, I want you to start brainstorming. Find a subject matter that appeals to both of you. Your project is due to me in a month, so time is of the essence."

That got my attention; panic welled up in me again. Could we really do this?

"I will leave you two alone. Please take the next half hour or so to talk, flip through the papers and magazines on the table, discuss potential subjects. I'll be over there if you need anything." Teni left us alone, her soft feet shuffling along the tile floor, skirt flowing around her long, lean legs.

We stood there awkwardly for a solid minute. Finally, Matthew cleared his throat and held out his hand. "So, I'm Matthew," he said.

I rolled my eyes. "I know who you are."

That crooked grin lit up on his face, and my stomach gave a funny pinch. "Just trying to start us off on the right foot. My mom would ground me if she found out I wasn't remembering my manners."

I reluctantly shook his hand. It was warm, strong, engulfing mine. Tanned skin mingled with my dark flesh. I tucked my hands in the pockets of my shorts and fought the tingle in my fingers. "Um, so do you have any ideas?"

Matthew sat down at a stool, his long legs splayed out in that casual effortlessness that sports guys always had. "Not a thing." Even his voice had a smile in it. "You?"

I perched on the stool beside him. "Nothing."

We each grabbed a magazine and began flipping through the pages. My eyes were on the pages, but every other sense was aware of Matthew. The soft rhythm of his breathing. The light, crisp scent of his cologne. The memory of his fingers touching mine.

"Nature?" he asked, showing a spread of a forest.

I shrugged. I didn't have anything against the outdoors, but it didn't call to me.

"What do you do when you're not here or working at the bakery?" he asked.

"Um, I hang out with friends." Study. Other nerdy things.

"Any hobbies?"

I arched a brow. "Other than art?"

He held up a hand in mock surrender. "Just trying to get to know you. To see if we can figure out something—"

"In common," I supplied. If I had a dollar for every time I'd heard that over the last couple of days, I'd be rich by now. "Well, I'm not into sports at all."

His lips thinned. "I'm not just a jock, you know."

My heart thudded. I'd insulted him without meaning to. "Sorry, I just—"

"I know what you think of me. Stupid, ignorant jock. How did he even get into this art program?" His words were quiet, but they echoed in my head like he'd screamed through a megaphone. "It's dangerous to make assumptions about people, especially ones you don't know."

He was right, I knew it, and it ticked me off how easily he read me. "Well, you're making assumptions about me," I countered.

"It's not an assumption. Your emotions are clear on your face—not too hard for anyone to read," he retorted. "I can tell you don't like me. You think I don't care about this as much as you do because I happen to spend most of my free time on the basketball court. Well, I worked hard to get into this program, just the same as you. I want to win this competition, just the same as you. We're gonna have to work together to make that happen. And the first step is to pick our subject."

With that, he turned his attention back to the magazine on his lap. I did the same, my stomach pitching. I couldn't see anything on the page, though.

I'd hurt his feelings. Made him feel like I thought I was smarter than him, through my disdain of pairing up with him, my distaste at his art style obviously evident. *My* mom would ground *me* if she knew how rude I'd been.

"I'm sorry," I said to him in a tone so low I wasn't sure he'd heard. I was afraid to look up, but I hoped he could feel the sincerity in my words.

A long minute passed.

"Apology accepted."

The band around my chest eased up a touch. I dared a glance at him and saw his gaze fixed on me, magazine in his lap forgotten. I couldn't read the emotion in his eyes, but he didn't seem quite so angry anymore.

One small step forward. A tiny one, yes, but important nonetheless.

Chapter ⬤ Six

Charlie dunked his head under the pool surface, then darted back up, shaking his head like a wet dog. Splatters of water smacked me in the face, and I grimaced.

"Knock it off or I'm taking you home," I warned him. The pool was already overcrowded, since it was hot but not unbearable outside. I was floating in the deep end, enjoying the crisp coolness of the water.

This morning Mom had asked if I'd get Charlie out of the house. He and Maxine had been holed up in the basement for days, working on upgrading their solar-powered car. She wanted him to drop the mad-scientist gig and just be a kid for a while. So I'd agreed to take them both to the pool.

It would also give me a bit of a reprieve from my anxiety

about the art project . . . and my guilt over how I'd acted toward Matthew. I'd lain in bed last night, embarrassed about how rude I'd become. Just because I didn't like the guy didn't mean I had to be nasty.

Though in truth, that wasn't quite accurate. It wasn't that I didn't *like* him. I actually didn't know anything about him except that we were really different. And if I were honest, part of my problem was that I was really uncomfortable.

Matthew's art challenged me. Made me squirm. It wasn't lovely or careful or familiar. It wasn't concerned with exacting perfection. It was wild and dark and edgy, and I didn't know how to handle it.

"Hey, Corinne," Charlie said, interrupting my thoughts. He dropped his voice and floated over to me, then peeked over both shoulders. "I . . . need to talk to you about something weird that happened." His face turned beet red.

Intriguing. I raised an eyebrow and reached my hand over to grip the edge of the pool, kicking my feet in a lazy pattern to keep me afloat. Water splashed on my back when a kid jumped in the water, but the lifeguard's whistle and shout stopped that.

"What's up?" I asked him.

He cleared his throat, looking around again. "It's about Maxine."

The subject of his discussion was currently talking with a couple of other neighborhood girls near the shallow end of the pool. Her dark brown hair was plaited in a thick braid and she wore a one-piece swimsuit, her golden legs thrust out on the steps.

"What about her?"

His back stiffened. "She . . . When we were working on our car, she . . . touched my hand."

I smothered a laugh. I *knew* it. This had been brewing for a long time now. Charlie was finally becoming aware that Maxine liked him, and he was totally in over his head. "I've touched your hand before."

He wrinkled his nose. "That's different. You're my sister."

"But she's your friend—has been forever. You two used to hold hands all the time when you were little. What makes you so worried about it now?"

"I dunno." He shrugged. "It just . . . felt different. She's been acting weird, too. Asking me if I like any girls, or if I thought her hair looked pretty in that braid today."

Charlie's lips were thinned, and he kept swallowing. Aw, the guy was so nervous. He could sense change happening in their relationship. I actually felt bad for him—once you crossed that line from friend to potential boyfriend/girlfriend, it wasn't easy to go back.

"Maxine is growing up," I started in a gentle voice. "She's looking at things differently, and that includes her relationship with you. Try to keep an open mind and think about it all."

"Do you think . . . she likes me?"

It took everything in me not to say, *Duh!* Instead, I nodded. "I think she's starting to go in that direction. But really, would it be that bad if she did? You guys are best friends. You know each other, and you get along well." I could see the protest on his face and continued, "Before writing her off, just think about it. Don't do anything rash right now—you'll just push her away."

"Hmm." He didn't seem convinced.

I pushed off the wall and floated in the water. "Just try to think about how you feel."

"About what?" a light voice said from behind me. Maxine tilted her head and smiled widely.

Charlie's face could fry an egg, it was so red from his blush. "Nothing," he muttered and pulled out of the pool. He stomped off, dripping puddles of water under his feet as he beat a hasty retreat.

Maxine's brow furrowed, and the smile slid from her face. "What did I do?"

I reached over and squeezed her shoulder. "It's not you, promise. My brother is a doofus. He's just . . . trying to sort stuff out." I knew exactly what was wrong with him. He'd sorted Maxine into one category—friends—and was jarred at the possibility of her being something else—a potential girlfriend. So he was being stubborn and refusing to give her a chance. Because he was scared.

Maxine gave a weak nod and a shaky smile. "I don't want him mad at me. I'm gonna go talk to him." Before I could reply, she tugged herself out of the pool and traipsed along after him.

Kids. I shook my head and lolled in the water. Though there was a small flare-up of something in my stomach as I considered Maxine and Charlie. I recognized some of myself in Charlie, that stubborn refusal to change my opinion of a person, despite the situation.

But our situations were completely different. Those two had been friends for years. They already had a foundation. All I had was an unwanted attraction to Matthew, and a lot of fear.

I shook off those thoughts and floated along the water, determined to enjoy my afternoon as best as I could. Twenty minutes later both Maxine and Charlie came back to the pool. Her eyes were red and streaked, and Charlie's face was unreadable.

"I'm ready to go home," he declared.

I glanced at both of them. Their bodies were wound so tightly I was sure they were going to explode. But neither offered an explanation of what had happened. "Okay, let me towel off and slip on my clothes," I said.

My heart squeezed for their obvious angst as I dried off and put my shorts and T-shirt back on. We walked in awkward silence the whole way home, with me in the middle. When we reached our house, Maxine gave me a quick thank-you and kept going to hers, not even looking back at Charlie.

"What happened?" I whispered to him once we made it inside. The cool air was a welcome pleasure, and I shivered as goose bumps formed on my bare skin.

He huffed. "She tried to kiss me. Can you believe it?"

I would have laughed had I not seen the sheer confusion and wariness in his face. It was hard for him to open up and tell me these things, and if he thought I was laughing at him, it would just shut him down. "She really likes you," I said quietly. "If you don't like her like that, you need to tell her before it ruins your friendship."

Charlie sighed and looked down at the carpet. "We can't just go back to how things were before, can we?"

"There is no going back, Charlie. I'm sorry."

He gave a miserable nod, his face pinched. Then he went into his room and closed the door behind him.

I grabbed a soda and plopped into the kitchen chair. Poor Maxine. Poor Charlie. I hoped they could work it all out. I pressed the cool can against my still-warm cheeks and sighed at the bite of coldness on my skin.

My mind kept taunting me with the vision of bold blue eyes.

A soft brush of fingers across the back of my left arm stopped me before I entered the art studio on Friday. "Hey, Corinne." It was Matthew right behind me, looking at me with cautious eyes. "Sorry, didn't mean to startle you. Just wanted to catch you before you went in."

My heart stopped for a painful moment, then restarted at an irregular pace. I had to admit, Matthew was looking good today. He had on faded jeans and a slim-fit black tank top that accentuated all those basketball muscles in his arms and shoulders. "Um, sure," I managed to say, wishing I sounded more suave. "What's up?"

He sighed and raked a hand through his hair. Another studio

student walked by, eyeing the two of us with evident curiosity. He dropped my arm. "I know this isn't your ideal situation. It's not quite ideal for me either, but I think you and I can put that aside and work together. Without all of this silence and awkward tension between us. Otherwise, it's never going to happen."

I bit my lower lip. His eyes darted down to my mouth and then away to stare over my shoulder. For some reason, that one small look made my skin flush.

I shoved aside that reaction and forced myself to focus on what he was saying. He was right—I knew it, and a big part of the problem here was my own stubbornness. We were both forced into a situation we hadn't envisioned. But if we were going to win, we needed to put aside our feelings, roll with the punches, and make an art project that was champion worthy.

Surely I could put up with him, with this . . . whatever between us, long enough to win, right?

I tilted my head. "So what do you want to win for? What do you hope comes out of this?" I knew what I wanted—fame, glory, all that jazz. But what was his purpose here? He seemed determined for us to work together, which meant he must want this for some big reason.

Matthew cleared his throat, his face showing an emotion I couldn't quite pin. "I have a few different reasons," he hedged, then glanced down at his watch. "Hmm, class is getting ready to start in a minute."

His nonresponse intrigued me. For someone who seemed

pretty open and easygoing, Matthew totally just blew off my question. Why?

I suddenly wanted to find out.

I raised an eyebrow and gave him a small smile, thrusting out my hand. "I'm in." No looking back now. I had no idea how we were going to make this work, but in this moment, that didn't matter. We wanted to win, and I was determined we'd make that happen.

He took my smaller hand into the warmth of his larger one. Our handshake looked professional, but all of my skin cells were suddenly hyperaware of him. The firmness of his thumb and fingertips, the lean line of his fingers.

It took everything I had not to yank my hand from his, which would totally defeat the purpose of our truce. But I'd never had a reaction to someone else like this before. Had never touched a guy's hand and wanted to lean closer to him, take a good, close look at all those little flecks in his riveting blue eyes.

What was going on with me?

I gave an embarrassed laugh and extracted my hand, fighting the urge to cram it into my shorts pocket. "Um, okay. I'm going to head inside now. For class. Our art thing." Wow, could I sound any dumber?

Luckily for me, he didn't seem to notice. "Sure. I figured that over the weekend, we can make a list of the subject matter that interests us most. Then on Monday we can work on narrowing down our options, plus what media we want to use."

He sounded so cool and collected, not frazzled like me. For some stupid reason, my chest tightened. Obviously I was the only one in turmoil here over this handshake, the only one feeling this weird buzz whenever we were close. So embarrassing.

"Sounds good," I said, lifting my chin and nodding. I straightened my back and walked inside. And for the entire class session, I kept my attention studiously on my project and not on Matthew.

And I would have been proud of that accomplishment too, had I actually been able to keep his crooked smile off my mind for more than five minutes at a time.

Chapter ● Seven

'd like a half pound of salami . . . a pound of bacon—thickly sliced, please—and a pound of turkey. Make those slices thicker, because last time I came here, they were falling apart in these tiny shreds." Mr. Stein shoved his thick gray-framed glasses up his nose with a gnarled, wrinkled hand as he peered across the glass case at me.

It was Saturday afternoon, and I was working the deli counter at the bakery. Mr. Stein was one of our regulars, and he was very particular about what he wanted. For some reason, though, he liked me and always wanted me to take his order.

I gave him a serious nod. "Sure thing, Mr. Stein." Then I went to work, slicing and weighing and bagging the items. I popped the price stickers on them and handed the packs over. "Anything else I can get for you?"

He thinned his lips as he perused the deli case again, running a hand over his bald head. "Maybe a half pound of that tortellini. Margie really loves it. She can have some with dinner."

Margie was his granddaughter, a sweet little girl with the biggest, fluffiest curls I'd ever seen. Every time she came in with Mr. Stein, I wanted to pick her up and squeeze her tight. She was so. Stinking. Cute.

I scooped out a half pound, stickered it, and handed it to him. "Have a great day," I said with a big smile.

A group of several chattering women walked through the door, and they kept me busy for another good fifteen minutes, running around and slicing, scooping, bagging, stickering deli goods. My feet were starting to ache in my flats. How did Grandpa do this every day?

I waved good-bye to the last customer and collapsed in a chair behind the deli counter, stretching my aching arches out in front of me and rotating my ankles. Then I grabbed my notebook and pen and stared at my nearly empty list.

The one I was supposed to have filled out by Monday to share with Matthew after class.

I only had two items so far of possible art subjects for us to do: an outdoor scene at a park, and a portrait of someone. I mean, what else could we possibly find that we would both want to work on, that we had in common? I knew I was supposed to list all the things I *wanted* to do, but I couldn't stop wondering what we could actually succeed at. So I was trying to focus my list on those subjects.

And it was paralyzing me.

Chewing on my pen cap, I tried to clear my mind and think about what could possibly work for contemporary and classical art styles. I rolled around different Cleveland locations in my head—maybe we could do something local. That could be intriguing. That old cemetery downtown? Lake Erie?

"Whatcha doin'?" Grandpa asked from beside me, and his voice startled me into opening my eyes. He had on a thin sweater—despite the temperatures outside, he kept it cool in the store.

I gave him a smile. "Artistic meditating." Or a desperate attempt to do so. If only I could clear my hectic mind and find that zone that allowed me to tap into ideas.

He grabbed another folding chair and plopped down beside me, dropping his large hands on his knees. "So how's your art classes going? Still having fun with it?"

I nodded and put my pen in the coil of my notebook. "It's been challenging so far. Trying different media, different techniques. Our instructor isn't going easy on us, but that's what I wanted. That's how I'll grow and achieve my goals."

Until Matthew totally came along and interfered with all of my plans. Accidentally, of course—it wasn't like he was trying to thwart me or anything—but I'd had everything mapped out about how the summer was going to go down. Now my brain was a pile of mush and I couldn't stop thinking about his smile or the way he'd touched my hand. Ugh.

Ava had teased me all last night when she came over for dinner and a movie at my house. Apparently I wasn't doing a good job hiding my turbulent emotions.

"Whatcha writin' there?" he asked, nodding at my notebook. "Homework?"

"Kinda." I filled him in on the details about the competition, fingers absently playing with the pen as I talked. "So now I have no idea what we can do. Our styles are so different—*we're* so different. I promised to put aside my concerns and do my best so we have a real chance at winning this competition, but I don't know how." A new sense of bleakness filled me.

I'd never been this pessimistic about stuff before. Why was this chewing at me so hard, making me so nervous? I was normally the one who gave it everything, despite the odds. I had a winner's mentality. I set goals and I accomplished them.

But this felt different. Much more emotional, in a strange way. Like there was more on the line than just the end prizes.

Grandpa rubbed his chin. "You know, your grandma and I were like that. Very different people. I was into art and baking and making beautiful things. She was a business woman. Also an activist, attending rallies about women's rights and equal pay." He smiled, closing his eyes for a brief moment. "I loved watching her in action. Getting fired up about those things that were important to her. She had so much passion."

He stood and moved over to the deli counter, straightening up the metal buckets holding the pasta. I put my notebook in the chair and got up too—if he was cleaning, that was my cue to do the same. I grabbed a paper towel and started wiping down the countertop.

"How did you guys meet?" I asked. I didn't know a lot about their relationship, since he was pretty closemouthed on details, preferring to keep them to himself. The fact that he was talking now was surprising, and I didn't want to let the moment go.

He sighed and wiped up a small mess around the chicken salad. "We were young. Too young," he said, throwing me a warning look.

I laughed. "I'm not dating anyone yet, Grandpa."

"Glad to hear. He has to be the right person. Someone good enough for my granddaughter."

The door dinged, and I pasted on my polite work smile. Grandpa went over to the bakery counter across from me and got a couple of dozen doughnuts for the harried-looking woman. She thrust forward a bunch of cash and ran out the door, boxes in hand.

"Some kind of doughnut emergency, I guess," he said with a chuckle as he came back to me. "Anyway. I had returned to Ohio after studying at the patisserie in Paris. What a wonderful experience that was. I was excited to start my own bakery. Your grandmother was doing some kind of political polling and had come in here because she was parched and wanted a soda—we'd only been open a few weeks at that point, actually. And the rest is history."

"But . . . you said you guys were different. How did you make it work out?"

Grandpa stopped cleaning and looked at me. "If you want something bad enough, you make it work. Don't get me wrong—I was plenty scared. She and I didn't see eye to eye on a lot of stuff. Those first years were all about compromising. We fought quite a bit as we learned how to deal with each other. But love made us keep trying."

I'd never seen Grandpa's face so open before. It was obvious he still loved and missed her, though the bittersweet smile he gave me showed he had no regrets. That at least he'd had time with her—a long time, at that.

I pursed my lips, considering his words. Grandma had always been vocal, pushing me to do everything I wanted to, even as a young kid. I remembered the way she smelled, like soft linen and sunshine. How she'd braid my hair and tell me I was smart and was going to be somebody. She'd inspired me; I'd wanted to make her proud.

Somehow, the two of them had compromised—and not just on an art project or something temporary. On life. In love.

Love. The word brought a hot flush to my face. I didn't have time for infatuations, much less love. But that didn't mean a small part of my heart didn't leap whenever Matthew jumped into the front of my mind. Which was all the time now. Or when I happened to glance at him as he worked on his projects in class—the careful focus and diligence in his art was magnetic. It was ridiculous, I knew, but I couldn't help my reaction.

He drew me to him, despite how hard I fought it. How hard

I tried to keep this just about one project. There was something in his eyes that made me want to get to know him more. Did he feel the same way about me, too?

Grandpa went to the back to bring out fresh supplies from our fridge. His eyebrow shot up as he peered over at me. "You have that look on your face," he said.

I fought the urge to press my hands to my heated cheeks. That would declare me as guilty. "I don't have any look. I'm just wondering how I can make it work out with Matthew on our project. Do you have any ideas for what our subject can be?"

His eyebrow rose higher but he didn't comment on my blatant lie. "I'm sure it'll come to you, honey. Just try to relax and invite inspiration in."

I nodded. The door rang again, and a steady stream of customers filtered in, keeping me busy for another solid hour. Not busy enough to stop my brain from whirring while I worked, however.

Okay. This was getting ridiculous. Matthew was cute—I'd already admitted that to myself. But he and I weren't going to fall for each other or anything. It was just one project. A summer thing. When school started again, I'd go my way and he'd go his. And hopefully we'd come out of it all with an art show win. My goals . . . I just needed to keep my focus. Eyes on the prize.

Grandpa appeared from the back, holding my cell phone; apparently he'd fetched it from the back room. "It just dinged," he said right after I finished serving the last customer in the crowd crush. "Figured it might be important."

Who was trying to reach me? Everyone knew I was working Saturdays here. I peeked down at it. A text message from a number I didn't recognize.

Hey, it's Matthew. We should figure out a regular time outside of class to meet for our project. When?

My heart did a thud-skip, and I could feel my cheeks burning. I'd given him my cell number after class yesterday, but I hadn't expected to hear from him so soon. My fingers were shaking as I typed out, **Tuesdays and Thursdays r good for me. U?**

"Is that him?" Grandpa asked with a knowing smile. "The boy you're working with in the class?"

I caught myself before I rolled my eyes at his smarmy look. "Yes, it is. He wants us to meet to work on our project. That's all."

My phone buzzed.

Those days work for me too. See u Monday. :-D

I handed Grandpa back my phone, trying to breathe normally. Like this was just your average run-of-the-mill conversation, not something I was nervous about. "It's not a big deal," I continued. "We're just art partners. That's all."

"You keep telling yourself that, Corinne," he said with a sly wink as he went into the back room.

"Look, Maxine—it's working!" Charlie pointed in excitement as the sun hit their sleek wooden car's solar panel, and the car went whizzing down the sidewalk.

Maxine gasped and gave him a high five, the sun glinting off the light brown highlights in her hair. "Yes! I knew it would."

I laughed and shook my head, shifting on the warm wooden bench. Apparently the scandal of the stolen kiss at the pool was water under the bridge. There was no lingering awkwardness between them right now, so Charlie must have decided to let it go. Which was good, because they'd been friends for so long. I hated to see things awkward with them.

Just before I was leaving to meet Matthew at the park, Charlie and Maxine had come into the living room, begging me to let them go too. They claimed they needed the vast open space offered in the park, as opposed to the busy residential street where our house was. I'd reluctantly agreed.

Truthfully, watching them run around gave me something to focus on while my stomach fluttered with masses of butterflies. My palms hadn't stopped sweating, and it wasn't just because of the warm weather.

"Are you watching?" Charlie called out to me with a wave. He and Maxine were probably fifty feet away now. "Did you see how far the car went? It just shot down the sidewalk!"

"Good job," I called out in response.

My gaze skittered away from them and moved across the park, searching out Matthew. I whipped out my notebook and stared down at it, looking at my list. I'd tried to let it go and let inspiration come to me, as Grandpa had suggested, but after spending a half hour staring at the ceiling, listening to classical music, I had to admit it wasn't working.

So I went online and looked at my favorite art websites, plus checked out events happening around town. My list now included the pier in downtown Cleveland, a few local festivals—sure to be rich with people watching—the cultural gardens on the east side, and the Metroparks. Surely we could find something among those we agree on. And if not, there was always his list.

I glanced up to see the object of my thoughts striding toward me with a slow, confident walk. When our eyes connected, his smile deepened and a dimple flared. The wind teased his hair, fluttered it in the breeze, and I itched to touch it.

My heart squeezed in response, and I swallowed.

Oh boy, I had a suspicion that I was so in over my head.

Chapter ● Eight

Y ou made it," Matthew said, giving me a wide smile. His teeth sparkled, and I found my own smile growing in response.

"Well, we have work to get done," I said, trying to regain my businesslike persona. I wasn't here to flirt or to admire how his shorts and T-shirt made his lean body look even taller. Nope, I was keeping my focus.

He nodded and slipped onto the bench beside me. Heat radiated from his body, only a few inches from mine. He grabbed a small notebook and tugged it out of his pocket, flipping a few pages in. "So, I have a list of ideas," he said.

I handed him mine, then looked his over. Even his penmanship was confident—solid letters. Not hurriedly scrawled, but purposeful. I blinked and made myself read the actual words.

My brow furrowed as I moved down the list. He'd put down stuff like city hall, an abandoned set of train tracks, a homeless shelter, a large hospital on the east side. The twist in my stomach grew a little tighter. Where was the beauty, the art in those things? There was nothing on this list that appealed to me.

I drew in a few steady breaths and dared a glance at him. His face was unreadable, eyes fixed on my list. He looked up, and I noticed a few small freckles on the bridge of his nose.

"Hmm. Our lists are . . . very different," he offered.

"We have nothing even close to being in common." I almost wanted to laugh because of how absurdly different our thoughts were. It would be hilarious, if there wasn't a lot on the line. "Ideas?"

"Okay." He tilted his head, thinking. "Is there anything on my list that you don't absolutely hate?"

I was unable to hide the small sigh as I looked back down at it. "Um . . . I guess the train tracks isn't too bad. But the rest of it isn't quite . . ." My words stalled. How did I put it without sounding like an art snob? What would Ava say? "The rest isn't what I would enjoy working on. It's not my personal style."

Matthew's lips thinned, and he quietly took the list from my hand. "Have you ever considered working outside of your style? I know you're not a modern art fan, but there's a lot of it out there that will change you, make you see the world differently. If you give it a try."

Something about his words made embarrassment burn in my chest. Was it my fault that I didn't like his style? I jutted out my jaw and crossed my arms. "It might be easier to connect with work if it wasn't a bunch of random splatters on a piece of paper, or a canvas with colored blocks. How is that supposed to 'change' me? What worldview will that give me, huh?"

He narrowed his eyes and offered me back my notebook. "Corinne, have you ever been to a contemporary art gallery?"

I shook my head. "No offense to you and your style, but nothing about that appeals to me. I stare at those pieces and see nothing, feel nothing. Some of them look like they were painted by a baby." Okay, that was a bit of a low blow, but how could he deny the truth in my words? Blunt, but honest.

Matthew stared at me so long I started to squirm. The sun beat down on the top of my head, and a line of sweat dribbled down my face. I resisted wiping it away, not wanting in that moment to look weak.

Then he startled me. A rich, warm laugh poured from his mouth. "You don't hold anything back, do you?" he said, mirth dancing in his blue eyes.

My jaw loosened a bit, and I gave a small smile, the tightness in my chest easing up as well. "I have a lot of strong opinions. But I think most artists do."

Matthew watched a small drop of sweat slide down my neck. I swallowed, frozen in place. There was a curiosity in his eyes as he raked his gaze over my face, really looking at me like it was the first time he'd ever seen me. I'd never felt so thoroughly . . . studied. "I think the problem is you've not been exposed to a lot of contemporary art. Yes, there is some like the stuff you're talking about. I admit it—I don't understand it all. Nor do I think I'm supposed to," he continued in a rush when I opened my mouth to reply.

"Then what's the purpose?" I asked, this time out of genuine curiosity, not hostility.

Charlie and Maxine ran through the grass in front of us, breaking the strange thread of connection building. Good. I needed a moment to pull back from this intensity. Regain myself.

"Sometimes the purpose is for us to interpret the work as we see fit. From our own perspective. We're not always supposed to 'like' it. But it makes us think." Matthew's words were quiet but powerful, and he turned his attention to stare off at the park. There were a group of teen guys playing on a basketball court now, laughing and shoving each other. Was he wishing he was out there instead of with me?

"I challenge you," I suddenly said, surprising even myself.

His head whipped around, and a fresh openmouthed smile broke out on his face. He raised an eyebrow. "A challenge?"

I thrust my chin in the air and gave him my most intense, serious look. "You show me anything that can compare to the classics, anything that really moves me the way the old artists' works do, and I'll eat my words." I didn't know why I said it. Did I really want to be changed? Possibly. But something about the passion with which he spoke about art moved me. I wanted to feel that.

Or at least try.

I loved art. But my love was safe, comforting. Classical art was like a warm blanket on a stormy day. It soothed my soul.

Matthew spoke of art like it was a forest fire.

"Fine." He crooked a smirk at me. "I accept that challenge. I hope you're ready to eat your words."

I swallowed, and my heart began its irregular thump-thump. Oh boy, was I ready for this? Too late to back out now. Pride made me give a shaky nod.

"There's a gallery right here in Lakewood that we'll go to on Thursday instead of meeting about our project," he continued. Excitement filled his voice, and he grabbed his phone and opened his notes program to jot something down. "I'll take care of it."

"Corinne!" Maxine hollered as she ran toward us. She was breathless and panting, her hands thunked on her knees as she bent over and drew in sharp breaths. "I think . . . Charlie lost . . . the car. It rolled . . . into a creek."

I sighed and stood. "I'd better go help him or he'll whine for a week about it."

Matthew nodded, and an emotion crossed his face that I couldn't quite pin down. He scrawled down an address on a scrap of paper and handed it to me. "Thursday. Eleven a.m. Meet me here."

I was proud of how steady my hand was when I grabbed the paper, even as his thumb brushed against mine. Small tremors zinged through my skin, but I don't think he noticed.

Matthew walked away, and I turned my attention to trying to save the solar car. But in the back of my mind, all I could think about was how my stomach would probably never be normal around him again.

The exterior was nothing like I expected. Thursday morning, I stood outside of the nondescript building on Detroit, a few cars flying by. There was a large picture window, a thick purple curtain hiding most of the interior from the outside world. The red front door had SANDS ART GALLERY written in a bold black script above it.

I glanced at the time on my phone. I was a few minutes early, so I leaned back against the brick wall, crossing my arms. I had on a flowing white shirt with slitted sleeves—dressy but cute. I paired it with a pair of fitted black jeans and sparkly flats. Thankfully there had been a bit of a break in the temperature, and it was only in the upper seventies, so the cool breeze slipped down the road and caressed my bare skin.

I had no idea what to expect from today's gallery visit, but I hoped it would go okay. I'd told myself a hundred times that I was not going to make today awkward. I wouldn't be stubborn, would open myself up to the experience, even if I ended up not liking it. I'd presented the challenge, so I had to give him a fair chance.

It didn't help things, though, that I kinda sorta felt like this was a date. As dumb as it sounded, my stomach had been a tangled mess ever since I'd gotten up this morning. I was nervous and excited about seeing Matthew. Sharing with him something that was so important to me—art.

It would be good for our project, I told myself, to get my head out of that zone. We were tentative friends. Partners. We needed to learn how to appreciate each other's styles. Maybe he'd even be open to exploring classical art at the Cleveland Museum of Art with me sometime. All in the name of research, of course.

"You look great," Matthew said, popping up beside me out of nowhere.

I jumped and pressed a hand to my chest, trying to steady my breathing. "You scared me to death!" I chastised.

"Sorry." The wicked twinkle in his eye wasn't the least bit sorry.

I rolled my eyes. "Let's just go inside." My traitorous brain kept looping on his compliment, though.

When we walked in, the gust of air-conditioning was so strong I actually shivered in delight. Matthew held the door open to let me enter first. The room was dim but not overly dark. There was soft instrumental music playing in the background, and the whole building looked like one big open floor plan with small exhibits thrusting out in various spots on top of the hardwood floor. The brick walls were painted a soft beige, covered in paintings of all sizes.

Matthew touched my lower back, and I swallowed. "Um, wait right here," he said, nodding toward the attendant in the corner. "I'll be back in a second." He headed to the older man and gave him two tickets.

The guy nodded and smiled, peeking over Matthew's shoulder to look at me.

I waved.

Matthew headed back, smiling. "Okay, let's make our way around."

"You didn't have to buy my ticket," I said.

"I didn't—they were a gift for us."

"But—"

"Let's get going before the gallery closes," he said in a teasing but firm tone. "There are some pieces I want to show you."

We walked to the left. There was a metal sculpture near the corner, pieces and curves thrusting out everywhere.

"Okay," I said, pointing at it. "What's up with this?"

Matthew studied it for a moment. He walked around it, taking it in fully. His eyes were fixed on the brushed metal as he did a couple of loops. He peered down at the little plate on the floor beside it. "This piece is called *Tragedy*. The artist created it after she lost her father in the Vietnam War. Keeping that in mind, what do you see in here?"

My heart tweaked in sadness for her. I couldn't imagine how it was to lose a parent, especially in a war. My grandfather didn't speak much about that time period except to say it was difficult—someone he knew had gone into that war and come back a changed man.

I followed Matthew's earlier path and circled the piece a

couple of times. I studied all the juts and lines. Forced myself to really look at it and see how it made me feel. There was a cluster of spikes in one corner with a small teardrop-shaped curve coming off a particularly vicious-looking spike.

The piece made me feel . . . lots of emotions. The spikes were a little scary, to be honest.

"It makes me uncomfortable," I admitted. "All these sharp points at the bottom. Someone could get hurt on those."

"It makes me wonder how her dad died," he said. "Look at this section. It's almost the opposite of the spiky part."

I peeked on the other side. There was a sweep of curved lines here, hunched around each other. When I kept staring at it, I swore I could almost see the arched back of a person, legs folded under.

Grieving.

"The spikes are her anger, right?" he said. "Her dad died in such a violent way. At war. And here she's crying for him."

I swallowed. "How do you know?" I asked him. It sounded plausible, and looking at the art, I could see how that would be an interpretation. But who was to say it was the right one?

"Well, that's the way I see it," he replied. There was no embarrassment, no wavering in his voice. "But someone else in a different place might see it another way. What do you see?"

I had to admit, after he pointed all of that out to me, the artwork started to come to life. The teardrops on top of the spike. The rubble on the ground, like artillery shells. It was like nothing I'd ever experienced before.

I licked my lips and stared at him over the top of the sculpture. "I never would have seen that if you hadn't pointed it out."

He shrugged, giving a shy smile. "Doesn't mean you wouldn't have seen something. And next time you see this piece, it might look different to you." He stepped around and grabbed my fingers, and I almost stumbled from the feel of our skin, from holding hands. "There's more I want you to see."

Matthew stayed close to me and took me to several of his favorite pieces. I could tell he'd been here a few times by the way he gushed about them. His enthusiasm was infectious. Though some of the stuff went right over my head, especially the one with doll heads glued to plastic cups.

"My brother could make that in five minutes," I said with a snort, staring down at the "art" resting on a low table. "What could this possibly be saying?"

"Look closer. What do you notice about these doll heads?"

I furrowed my brow and scanned down the row. There had to be a hundred blond heads stuck in the cups. Then I saw one in the very back corner. It was a black doll—the only one in the whole group of white dolls.

"This piece makes me angry," he said quietly. I heard the thread of strength in his voice. "There's a lot I see here. Race, of course—how monochromatic almost everything on here is. But also how fake and plastic we as a society have become." He glanced at me. "What does this make you think about?"

I blinked and rubbed a hand on my upper chest, right under

my throat. Once he pointed it out, a bunch of contrasting emotions fluttered in my stomach. I picked a memory that flew right to the front of my mind. "My mom gave me both black and white baby dolls as a little kid." I paused. "I've always been aware of race, of course. As a black girl, that's inevitable in our society. But the color of my friends has never mattered to my family."

He crooked a grin. "I bet you were a cute kid."

I shrugged. "I had a bit of a mouth. Always stubborn."

"I believe that."

I nudged him in the side, and he chuckled. Sometime over the last hour, the walls had slowly dropped between us. I could feel a difference already. Less hesitation when we spoke to each other. More honesty.

Matthew was smarter than I'd given him credit for. Way smarter. I'd seriously misjudged him, had assumed he was just a flake who didn't care about anything but sports. But he had lots of passion, and the skill to rouse that feeling in others. Even just walking around with him, I could feel his intensity about art.

Had I ever been that strongly vocal about anything I believed in?

Something about him sparked a feeling deep in my heart that I wasn't about to label yet. It made me uncomfortable, aware of myself, of him. All I knew was that despite my discomfort, I wanted to feel it more.

Chapter ●Nine

He and I walked a little more around the gallery wall in silence, taking in a series of similar paintings hanging on the far wall. They were a theme of colors. I stood there and just absorbed. Turned off my inner judgmental side and made myself stare at the image, let it present itself to me.

Then I noticed the pattern. The one square of red that made its way marching across the paintings. What did it mean?

I turned to him, expectant.

He laughed and held up his hands. "Hey, I don't have all the answers. This is a new installation since I've been here."

"How often do you come to this gallery?" I suddenly found myself wanting to know more about him. Who his family was, where he lived, what he did when he wasn't playing basketball or taking our class.

"As often as I can. At least a couple of times a month." He chuckled. "My uncle's girlfriend owns this gallery, so she lets me visit whenever I want. For free."

Interesting. "It's good to have connections," I teased. "Do you ever come here with anyone?" My face burst into flames when I realized how that could sound. "Um, I mean, like friends or family or whatever." *Wow, way to be weird, Corinne.*

He angled just a fraction toward me and peered down into my eyes. His pupils were wide and dark, and the irises were just a slim blue line around them. I saw him swallow. "You're the first person I've come here with." His voice was low but intense.

I drew in a steadying breath, my heart thundering in my chest. I'd sworn I wasn't going to give any further thought to this stupid, simple crush I had on him, but the way he was looking at me right now . . . I couldn't resist the pull.

I stepped just a hair closer; heat poured from his body. A small flutter at the base of his throat showed his heart rate matched mine.

"So glad to see you again, Matthew," a tall slender woman interrupted us. Her brown hair was pulled into a messy bun on her head and she wore a flowing dark blue dress.

I jerked in surprise but tried to recover my cool. Her scrutiny hit me in full force as she took me in with her eyes. Must be his uncle's girlfriend. I thrust out my hand. "Hi, I'm Corinne."

"Brianna, this is my art project partner," Matthew said smoothly, so much so that I wondered if I'd imagined that moment between us.

Her smile widened, and she shook my hand. "Glad to meet you. We heard about your project. Good luck in the competition!"

"Thanks," I said, keeping my attention off Matthew and firmly on her. "We're trying to get inspiration and decide what we're going to do our project on. We can't seem to agree."

"It can be hard," she said with a knowing nod. "But once you find your inspiration, I'm sure it will flow." She gave Matthew a wide, warm smile. "He's a smart one. You're lucky to be paired with him. He'll work hard, and he's truly gifted. Rare to see such profound talent in a guy his age."

Matthew's face turned a bright shade of crimson. "I'm no more talented than anyone else in our class." He cleared his throat and turned to me. "Teni has a piece on display if you want to see it."

The more time I spent around Matthew, the more I started to realize Brianna was right. There was something special about him—his perspective on the world, his intensity. It made me realize how very safe I played it. Because there was something safe about classical art. When you looked at a piece, you essentially knew what you were going to get. No big surprises—the image was clearly rendered on canvas with little to debate. Yeah, there might be symbolic layers in there, but the meaning of the paintings weren't greatly altered depending on who was looking at it.

I nodded and followed him to see Teni's bold-colored painting of two African girls. They wore simple dresses and had wide smiles on their faces, white teeth gleaming in golden sunshine. Somehow Teni had managed to blend the classic and the modern in her approach—I could see the girls clearly, knew what the subject matter was, but the unusual, varied lines that formed their figures gave the piece freshness. Matthew and I could definitely learn something from her.

I'd anticipated coming here and being bored, validated in my snobbery about contemporary art. But Matthew had challenged me to look beyond my initial disdain and give the pieces a chance. And in all honesty, as we stood side by side, staring at Teni's art, I was glad he had.

"What am I supposed to do while you're gone?" I whined to Ava as I tugged thin strips of her hair into small braids. "I'm going to be all alone, with no one to talk to about all of my angst."

She was currently sitting on the floor between my dangling lower legs while I sat on my bed. Ava stretched out her limbs, flexing her freshly painted bold blue toenails. "I'm sure you can find something to keep you distracted. Something starting with the letter *M*."

I tugged her hair a little harder than I needed to, and she gave a short howl. "Oh, I'm so sorry about that," I said sweetly.

"You're mean." She pressed fingers to her scalp and groaned like I'd ripped the hair out by the roots. "I'm going to be bald now. And then no Scottish boys will find me attractive. Thanks so much for ruining my plans."

My mom popped her head in the door and eyed me and Ava. Her eyebrow shot up when she saw Ava's head half-covered in rows of braids, but she wisely decided not to comment on it. Ava and I sometimes did weird things on our weekly sleepover nights, like experimenting with hairstyles or avant-garde fashion. A tradition we'd started back in middle school. "You girls need anything before your father and I go to bed?"

"No, Mrs. Walters," Ava said with a smile. "So long as your daughter stops ripping out all of my hair in revenge."

"Corinne, be nice," Mom chastised, then winked. "Okay, keep it down, ladies. Good night. Don't stay up too late, honey. You have to work tomorrow, remember?"

We echoed our good nights to her, and she closed the door.

I rolled my eyes and turned the music in the background down a fraction. It was only eleven, but my parents were already going to bed. Typical—I couldn't remember the last time they'd stayed up even until midnight. "What are your folks doing tonight? Are you guys all packed?" I made quick work of finishing her braids.

"Mostly. Just a few odds and ends left. It's going to be a lot of fun. I'll take a million pics and send them to you. My mom has international calling and unlimited data, so I can check in with you online." She tilted her head to look at me, giving me a pitying smile. "I'm sorry I was teasing you about Matthew. I know you're uncomfortable with the whole thing. But it sounds like going to the museum might have been good for you."

I slipped down to the floor beside her and rested my back against the bed. "It was. I mean, I'm stubborn and set in my ways. I know that. But I do want to make this work with him." I needed to win. And to be honest, there was a small part of me that was excited by the challenge of trying something different.

Pushing my craft, as Teni always said.

Well, if anything was going to nudge me out of my comfort zone, it would be working with Matthew.

"What was your favorite piece?" she asked me.

I scrunched up my face and thought about the whole gallery. After seeing Teni's piece, we'd lingered for another good hour, strolling around and taking it all in. Brianna had even brought us some tea to sip while we perused.

"Probably the wooden sculpture of the woman holding a child." I told her all about it. The carving was small, only a few inches around, and resting on a tall pedestal. But the moment I'd seen it, I'd wanted to touch it and see if the exterior was as smoothly polished as it appeared. The figures hadn't been immediately evident, but soon the gentle, flowing lines of the mother's back and the baby cradled in her arms had popped out at me. They were both faceless, but their bodies conveyed emotion anyway. Love. Nurturing.

Powerful.

"I'm proud of you," Ava said.

I blinked. "How so?"

"For keeping an open mind. It's easy to get caught in a rut and not take a risk on something else, especially when it comes to art." She snorted. "My mom refuses to decorate our house in anything but old-fashioned country décor. It kills my soul."

I laughed. It was true—her kitchen alone looked like it came straight off a farm. Red checkers, chicken statues, pig salt shakers . . . she went a little overboard. "Maybe in Scotland she'll find a style she likes better. Like plaid."

"I hope so. At least it would be different." Ava laughed and grabbed her soda, sipping. "How's your brother, by the way? Are he and Maxine still being weird?"

I'd told Ava about the pool kiss and then their strange makeup afterward. "Actually, they don't seem to be hanging out together as much. Charlie had invited her over for dinner tonight but she told him she had plans already. Poor guy seemed shocked that she wouldn't drop everything to hang out with him." I chuckled. "He pouted the whole meal in silence, then ran up to his room and stayed there."

Ava gave a sympathetic moan. "So he hasn't fully accepted that she likes him, huh? Even though she kissed him?"

"At this rate, Maxine would have to throw a brick at Charlie's head for him to wake up."

"I hope it doesn't come down to that," she teased. "I mean, your brother has a hard head and all, but . . ." She paused and grabbed a magazine off my bedside table. "Hey, let's do a quiz."

I finished braiding her hair as we spent the next half hour taking quizzes to find out our ideal careers, what kind of boyfriend was perfect for us, where would be our ideal vacation.

Ava laughed—the last quiz told her she should go somewhere with rich history, like England or Scotland. "I feel like I'm going to peak too young at this rate."

"At least you're going to experience it. Who knows when I'll ever make it to Italy." I sighed. "Can you imagine, being immersed in all of that artwork, hundreds of years old? The architecture, the food, the language."

What would be Matthew's ideal vacation spot? The thought popped into my mind unbidden. I swallowed and pushed it right back out of my head.

Ava gave me a wide grin. "You're thinking about him, aren't you."

I furrowed my brow. "What?" How did she know?

Her smile widened, and she laughed. "You got this soft look in your eyes, followed by this blush and then an angry scowl. Seemed the most logical explanation." She patted my arm and reached behind her head to grab one of the pillows off the bed, tucking it across her lap. "You'll be much happier if you stop fighting the way you feel and just accept it. There's nothing wrong with having a crush on Matthew."

"Easy for you to say." For as much of a crush as I had, there was also a healthy dollop of fear. Even if Matthew did like me in return, who was to say we'd work out? I'd seen plenty of couples start out strong but end with a horrible fight. Ava's last boyfriend, for example.

Because those differences that had drawn them to each other had eventually ripped them apart.

I didn't want that.

A pillow smacked me in the face. "No more moping," Ava said with a laugh as she jumped up.

I grabbed a pillow, grateful for the distraction. This was time to spend with my best friend, not to think about him. "Oh, the war is on now, girl."

Chapter ● Ten

I have seen notable progress in our skills as a whole over the last couple of weeks," Teni announced to our class on Monday morning. Her anklet jingled as she made her way up the aisle to the front of the room. Her long brown dress swished around her slender legs. "For every challenge I have given you, you have risen to the occasion and surprised me."

I could almost feel the proud smiles in our group. Our recent projects were hanging on display behind Teni in two rows. I had to admit, she was right. I could see a difference in my skills already, and there was a month left of classes. By the end of it, who knew where I'd be?

As Teni went on praising our talents, my gaze slid over to Matthew. He and I had talked on the phone last night for a good hour, trying to narrow down what our art project would be. Part of what had taken so long was that Matthew kept interjecting odd, random questions out of nowhere in the middle of the conversation, like, "What makes you angry?" "Ocean or lake?" and "What's your favorite type of metal?" He'd claimed there was a method to his madness.

Apparently he'd been right. After listening to my answers, Matthew had proclaimed that we should make Lakeview Cemetery our subject matter. One of the oldest cemeteries in the area, it would provide the rich history I loved with interesting architectural elements that appealed to him.

The perfect compromise for us. I had to give it to him; the guy had read me much quicker and easier than I'd read him. I'd only gone there once before on a school trip, but I remembered being awed by the mausoleums, the rolling hills of memorials. The area was serene, quiet. I'd always wanted to go back. It would be fun trying to capture that essence in a painting.

Now to figure out how we would combine our art styles.

Matthew's head turned toward me and he gave me a grin, blue eyes twinkling. Then he winked, of all things. My heart fluttered in response at being busted staring at him. Face burning, I jerked my gaze away and focused back on Teni, who was still talking.

"—going to initially seem easier than your last project, but don't underestimate the challenge," she said.

Crud, I was missing everything because of thinking about Matthew. I turned my full attention to her.

"Many famous artists have done extended studies in one color. Learning everything they can about it. Some have worked for years this way. So, the first thing I want you to do is decide which color you're going to work in. Then look around the room, look at magazines and books, whatever you need to get inspiration flowing so you can pick your subject matter."

The group spread around the room, milling in front of Teni's various displays of objects and such that are scattered on tables along the walls. I stayed on the outskirts, peeking over shoulders.

"I dare you to do your project in all white," a soft whisper spoke from behind me.

I spun around and gave Matthew a mock glare. "Okay. Then you do yours in all black. Let's see what Teni thinks of our artwork then."

"She'd probably think we were innovative."

"Or troublemakers."

"What color are you going to choose?"

I pursed my lips as I thought. "I dunno. Maybe red. You?"

He grinned. "Green."

Direct opposites on the color wheel. Of course. I shook my head, though a small wry grin creased my face.

"This is getting to be a dangerous pattern with us," he continued. "Picking opposites and such."

I moved an inch or two toward him. "I'm starting to suspect you're doing it on purpose," I said in a low, almost purring tone. Wow, was I *really* flirting with Matthew?

He leaned a fraction closer, and I stared, transfixed, at his magnetic eyes. They seemed to see everything in me, stripped past my words to see my core. The smile fell from his face and he said, in all seriousness, "Maybe I am, Corinne." Then he straightened, gave me an almost indiscernible wink, and walked away.

I sighed and watched him move to browse a table on the other side of the room, then shook it off and turned my attention back to class.

The next half hour went fast. I'd decided to use red as my color. What would be a great subject matter? What did red symbolize? I flipped through photo books and magazines, looking for an image that would capture the spirit of red.

I stopped at a page in National Geographic. There was a sunset over a lake in Africa, water rippling with vibrant reds and pinks. Illuminated by the setting sun was a lone giraffe, skin rosy as it stood beside a tall, scraggly tree. The animal's head was thrust proudly into the air, reaching for low-lying leaves, and a small baby giraffe stood right behind it.

Yes. This was it. I ripped the picture out—Teni was fine with us taking our inspiration back to our stations—and practically flew to my table. I was already planning out my piece. First step, draw the image.

I got so caught up in sketching out my initial rough draft that I almost didn't hear Teni dismiss the class. With a sigh, I got myself out of the art zone and put away my pencils and supplies.

Teni waved at me and Matthew. We made our way to the front of the room.

"So." She clapped her hands and beamed at us. "You have chosen your subject, yes? Tell me about it."

I explained to her our idea—that we'd choose one mausoleum in Lakeview Cemetery and split it in half on the canvas, each of us doing a different perspective of the same subject. "That way, we can each showcase our unique talents," I finished, looking to him for confirmation.

Teni remained silent for a moment, stroking her chin. "Hmm. That sounds . . . disjointed."

My stomach swirled. She didn't look too enthused about our idea. "What's wrong with it?"

"I'm not sure that's very cohesive," she slowly started. "The judges will be looking to see how well you two work together. Splitting a canvas clean in two may not necessarily show teamwork. But it may come down to execution."

Matthew remained silent. Was he as frustrated as I was right now? So hard to read.

I cleared my throat. "We'll make sure it's a cohesive piece," I promised. Somehow, we'd prove Teni wrong. She wasn't sure we could pull it off, but I knew we could.

We had to—there was no other option.

I hated it.

With a heavy sigh, I slammed my pencil down on my bedroom desk in disgust. Okay, hated was a bit too strong. More like I really didn't like how the competition piece was coming along. Technically it was clean—my lines were strong, and the perspective was accurate.

But the piece seemed flat. Lifeless. Dull.

Matthew and I had decided to each take half of the mausoleum. I had the top left corner, and he had the bottom right corner, with our lines meeting in the middle. We'd printed off two copies of the image to scale so we could ensure our images would be able to be cut and pasted together. All very planned out.

But it felt . . . wrong.

Was Matthew struggling with his part of the piece? Or was it just me? And what was *wrong* with me—why wasn't I able to get into this the way I normally could?

I put away my art supplies and plopped down on my bed, running my fingers along the soft bedspread. The walls seemed to close in on me. The room was too warm, too smothering. I needed fresh air. Air and perspective.

I grabbed my house keys and cell phone and crammed them into my shorts pockets. I closed my bedroom door behind me and hollered toward the kitchen, "Mom, I'm going for a walk."

"Got your phone?" she yelled back. I could hear her chopping something. "Make sure you're back in an hour. Dinner will be ready then."

"Yes, I have my phone. I'll see you in a bit!" I ran out the door before she could suggest I take my brother with me.

The late afternoon air was warm, cocooning me as breezes swirled the hem of my T-shirt and caressed my bare legs. My sandals smacked the concrete sidewalk. I had no idea where I was going. Just that I needed to find . . . something. I wasn't sure what that something was yet, but intuition was pulling me in this direction.

I turned right and headed west, toward the sun. It was warm but not unbearable. I adored summer—the freedom to spend my days as I wanted, not just studying, studying, studying. I loved school, of course. But sometimes . . . I wanted something else.

Independence, like this.

I walked a good mile until I hit an area of Lakewood where there was a stretch of tagged walls, boasting graffiti by various artists. I saw dirty, scuffed neon spray paint with peoples' names. Then I stopped.

Along the bottom of the wall, where brick met sidewalk concrete, there was a running motif. Someone had painted small vines and flowers, the partially fading colors stretching on and on. How had I never noticed that before?

I tugged my phone out of my pocket and snapped a shot. Then another. I played with lighting, zooming away, cropping. Then I pulled back and looked at the whole wall—really looked at it. Not just as destruction of property, the way I usually saw graffiti. But as someone expressing art. What did the piece say to me?

I studied the flowing lines, the cursive of the bright graphics. These weren't just slapped on in haste. The words were carefully rendered, no sloppy marks marring the image. The colors were red and black and green. I took more pictures—portrait, landscape. I angled myself so the sun washed the image in a rich haze and the letters were barely discernible.

When I flipped back through my pictures, I blinked. Some of them were actually quite good. I couldn't believe I'd taken them.

And suddenly, I wanted to find more. Things I would have dismissed as junk that could be re-envisioned as art. Walking another block, I saw an old glass bottle with a wilted daisy in it, resting on its side in the grass border on the curb. I took some shots of it.

An old scruffy dog with matted hair, lying on its side, who eyed me suspiciously as I neared.

A row of ants dragging pieces of cracker.

An abandoned apartment building with gaping teeth for windows and a boarded-up front door.

There was a strange bubble of excitement in my chest. Like I was seeing the world in a different way than I ever had before. I'd always found beauty in what was considered typically beautiful—attractive people, attractive buildings, attractive locales. Safe, steady.

Boring.

There was an artistry in the lines when I zoomed close and focused more on texture and shape instead of on capturing a lovely image.

Before I knew it, it was time for me to head back home. I peeked through my photo roll to my favorite shot, a pair of navy blue flip-flops that had been carefully placed on the edge of the sidewalk. Something about the image looked like the shoes' owner would walk by any second and slip her feet into them. Where were those shoes supposed to go? Why had someone left them here?

On impulse, I composed a text message to Matthew: **Are these yours? ;-)** Then I attached the picture and sent it before I could talk myself out of it. The instant it went, I wanted to take it back.

Maybe that was dumb. He might think it wasn't that interesting, might not see that moment of artistry I'd seen in the shot.

I tucked my phone into my pocket and, with the sun warming my back, headed back home.

When I turned onto my street, my phone buzzed, and I jumped a little in nervousness. My fingers shook as I tugged it out of my pocket.

Will check in when I get to Scotland! WHOO!

A text from Ava. I swallowed down the disappointment and felt a surge of shame. This was my best friend here. And I was getting hung up on some guy. I couldn't believe myself.

Can't wait! I texted her back. When I put my phone back in my pocket, I resolved to stop thinking about Matthew. It was a dumb, impulsive idea to send him the picture.

The cold air-conditioning smacked me in the face, and I sighed in bliss as I headed right to the fridge for a water bottle. As I helped Mom set the table, my thoughts were torn between wanting to look at my pictures again and wondering if Matthew was going to respond.

Chapter ⬤ Eleven

T his book is soooo boring," Charlie whined, rolling his eyes. He flopped the paper-back in his lap and arched back against the arm of the couch. "All these dwarves and little people stomping around, always singing, too."

I picked it up. *The Hobbit*. One of Charlie's summer reading books. "Oh, this one's great," I said. "Give it time. It will pick up. You'll want to read the rest of the books, I promise." I flopped on the opposite end of the couch from him, still full from dinner. Mom had made fried chicken, Brussels sprouts—which Charlie had adamantly refused to eat—and mac and cheese. I, on the other hand, had eaten everything, plus seconds.

My phone vibrated in my pocket. Ava must be bored. I tugged it out. Two texts, but not from her.

My missing shoes! LOL

U busy? Sorry I didn't reply earlier. Phone died.

I was pretty sure my heart literally stopped in my chest. He'd replied back—and had a legit reason for not writing me earlier. I managed to type out a casual, **Just chillin. U?**

"Who are you talking to?" Charlie leaned up against me, peering over my shoulder at my phone.

I jerked it out of view and scowled. "No one. Go back to reading your book."

He sulked and tossed the book on the coffee table.

"You'd better finish your reading for the day, bud," Mom hollered as she was coming down the stairs. "Or else you're gonna be grounded from video games tomorrow."

Charlie mumbled under his breath, then grabbed the book and tucked back into the corner. My brother was definitely not a reader. He liked action, not just sitting around.

My phone vibrated again. I looked down and it was Matthew, calling me this time. Oh God! Mom was coming into the living room any second now. I jumped off the couch and ran for the backyard, closing the door behind me. "Um, hello?"

"I really liked that picture," he said. His voice was warm and low, and it rolled over me.

I forced myself to play it cool, looking off into the setting sun past the houses behind ours. "Thanks. I was working on our project but it . . . just wasn't flowing for me." I was surprised I'd even admitted that to him.

He sighed. "Me neither. I keep trying to figure out what I'm doing wrong, but it isn't feeling right. Have any ideas?"

I sat down on a still-warm patio chair and kicked my feet up on the ottoman. "No clue. Maybe Teni can help." Though I was hesitant to admit to her that maybe she was right—whatever we were doing, it wasn't working.

"Maybe we need to regroup and try again. There's still time." He cleared his throat. "Um, so, maybe you could hang out with me for a while? You know, to discuss the project, of course."

A slow flush crawled up my throat and across my cheeks. His words sounded casual, but there was a thread of emotion there I'd have to be deaf not to pick up on. He was nervous. Which made me even more nervous . . . but also a little intrigued. Maybe I wasn't the only one suffering from this strange emotion? "Yeah, sure."

We ironed out a day and time—I'd meet him at a park by his house and we'd proceed from there. Then there was a lull in the conversation.

"So, what are you up to?" I asked, realizing I didn't know much about him. How he spent his free time. Surely it wasn't all art and basketball, right?

"Just hanging at home with my sisters."

"More than one?" I couldn't imagine having another Charlie running around the house. He was enough to handle, thank you.

"I have twin sisters who are getting ready to enter sixth grade in the fall. They're fun, but they can be a handful sometimes."

I smiled. "My brother will be in eighth grade. I feel your pain."

A breeze danced across my skin, and I settled into the cushion. The sun streaked purples and pinks across the sky as it descended. Sunset had to be one of the most beautiful times of the day.

"Where are you right now?" he asked.

"My back patio."

"I'm in mine, too, watching the sun set." His voice was quiet, slightly reverent. "I like how no sunset is ever the same."

Huh. It was true—there were always slight variations in the clouds, the way the light dispersed in the sky. "I never thought about it before," I admitted. There was something nice and intimate about sharing this moment with him.

"I liked your picture," he said again. "It was different from your usual art."

My cheeks burned. I couldn't dare to admit that he'd inspired me to look at the world differently. "Just trying to break free of my usual zone."

We talked for another minute or two until he said he had to go and break up a fight between his sisters. I laughed, and we hung up. I stayed on the patio for another few minutes, staring at the ever-darkening sky, my stomach twisted with nerves. I was simply anxious about having to rethink our project, I told myself. That was all.

It had nothing to do with the fact that I was also eager to see him again.

I was so early. I fidgeted on the bench and checked the time again. Still another twenty minutes before Matthew was going to arrive. The sky was a little overcast, so the sun wasn't beating down heavily on me. Which was good, because I was already sweating from nervousness. And my stomach wouldn't stop pinching.

So dumb. I'd been meeting with him regularly, so it wasn't like this was anything new. What had changed?

Me. Somehow, little by little, there was a shift happening in me. It was like my eyes were seeing everything for the first time. And I knew he was the reason why.

I stood, wiping my palms on my jeans. Maybe I could just meet him at his house instead of sitting here and psyching myself out. The walk would give me something to focus on. He'd mentioned on the phone that his house was at the back corner of the park, so I began strolling in that direction, looking for one with the backyard facing west.

I reached the edge of the park and crossed the street. In front of a small brick bungalow, two brown-haired, blue-eyed girls were whispering furiously from their spot on the front step. I could hear them hissing heated words at each other, pointer fingers waggling in each other's faces. One was dressed in shorts and a T-shirt, and the other in a pale purple dress. Had to be his sisters. Matthew had said they were named Jennifer and Carmen.

I smiled and walked up to them. "Hi, is this Matthew's house?"

The two girls were almost identical—I could barely discern a difference in their faces, except that one had more freckles on her nose. They both looked just like their brother, but with lighter, feminine features.

The girl on the left paused and eyed me. Then she smiled widely, showing a cute gap between her teeth. "You must be Corinne."

He'd talked about me? I swallowed and tried to maintain a calm facade. "Yup, that's me. I was supposed to meet him at the park but—"

"Matthew!" the freckle-faced girl stood and bellowed. "Your date's here!"

"Oh, no," I rushed to say. "Um, it's not a date. We're—"

"Hey, brother!" the first girl hollered. "Your girlfriend's waiting for you!" They turned to each other and tittered.

Nice. Luckily, I had a lot of training with annoying younger siblings. I just shot them a serene smile and ignored their teasing. They'd eventually get bored.

The front door whipped open, and Matthew barged outside, tugging it closed behind him. He stopped and blinked. "Oh, you're here." His cheeks flushed a tinge of light pink. "I thought we were meeting at the park."

Suddenly I felt self-conscious. It was evident by the tension in his body language that he didn't want to meet me here. But why? "Sorry," I mumbled. "I figured I'd just . . ." I shrugged my shoulders.

Shoving back my awkwardness, I scanned my gaze over the house. It was smaller than ours. The yard was tidy. The shutters were bright red, freshly painted. It was a cute place. Was he inse-cure about it?

Matthew came down the steps, long legs clad in faded jeans, wearing a soft gray shirt that I wanted to touch. I kept my hands firmly at my sides as he strolled up to me. The smile around his face didn't feel as warm as usual. "Sorry." He was just inches away from me, and I saw flickers of something in his eyes. "I'm just a little . . . self-conscious about our place. I've ridden my bike in your neighborhood before, and it's really nice."

My heart tightened a bit, and I suddenly wanted to assuage his concern. He was worried about the differences in our families' money. "Hey, it's fine. I'm sorry I put you on the spot. I was just a little . . . anxious waiting for you, so I decided to come here."

"Anxious about what?"

I swallowed, shrugged. "Um, just—"

"Matthew," a woman said from just inside the doorway, a dish towel slung over her shoulder. She was tall and brunette with a friendly smile. Apparently the hair color was passed on to every-one in the family. She eyed me with interest. "Who's your friend?"

He groaned and gave a good-natured eye roll. "She's my art partner. Corinne, this is my mom. She's very nosy."

I laughed. "It's nice to meet you," I said.

She waved at both of us. "Before you go out, why don't you have dinner here with us?"

"Oh, I don't want to get in the way," I said quickly. "I'm sure you guys already had plans." Obviously I'd interrupted them eating before he was going to meet me. The awkwardness came back full force, and I spun to head back to the park. "I'll just go back to our meeting spot and see you when you're done."

"That's okay," he said, stepping in front of me and waving me toward the door. The tension was still there in his body, but I could tell he was trying to be polite, which made me feel even more like a jerk. "Please, come on in. Did you eat already?"

I was tempted to lie and say I had, but I just made a noncommittal sound.

His mom smiled and practically shoved me in the door. "No one leaves my house hungry."

The twins laughed behind me. "That's true," one of them offered. "Mom feeds pretty much everyone in the neighborhood."

The house was nice and cool on the inside, with lots of light and color. Throw pillows covered a small tan couch, and the walls were bright blue in the living room. There was a small TV tucked into the corner with a pile of DVDs beside it. The place was clean; it was obvious his family took care of what they had.

"I can go," I whispered to him. "Seriously, it's okay." Yes, my parents made a decent income, but I didn't want him to feel like I was comparing our houses or anything.

A look crossed his face, and the tension leaked out of his body. "No, I'm sorry. I'm just . . . we don't have a lot of money, and I never have guests over here." He gave a genuine smile this time. "My mom's gonna make you look at pictures of me."

"Little kid pictures? Sounds like blackmail time." I laughed.

"Corinne, come over here!" his mom said, waving at a shelf bearing dozens of framed photos. "Look at these shots of Matthew as a kid."

He groaned. "Told you."

One of the twins thrust a picture in front of my face. "Check this one out. Matthew in the bathtub!"

He tried to grab it, but she giggled and waved it away from him.

His mom plucked it out of the air. "Girls, don't embarrass your brother. Anyway, it's time for dinner. We can look at pictures later." She smiled at me. "I hope you brought your appetite. I made extra."

I shot a glance at Matthew. His eyes were slightly hooded but he was staring at me with real interest.

"I'd like you to stay. If you want to, that is," he said softly.

There was no way I could resist those gentle words. "Okay."

Chapter ● Twelve

Mom, Jennifer won't hand the bread basket over," Carmen said in a tone that sounded exactly like my brother's. Her freckled face was twisted in an angry pout.

I smothered a laugh.

Matthew, who was sitting beside me, leaned over slightly to whisper in my ear. "They've always had a love-hate relationship with each other. Right now it's in the 'hate' phase. They're refusing to dress alike, despite most of their wardrobe matching until the last month or so. Jennifer's even talking about cutting her hair and making it darker."

Goose bumps erupted across my skin from the soft puffs of his breath on my ear and neck. I tried not to shiver and give anything away. We'd only been sitting at the table for a few minutes, but I was so tuned in to everything about him that it was ridiculous. I could feel the heat pouring from his thigh, just an inch or two from mine.

It was hard, trying to focus on the polite conversation his mother was making. But I'd learned that Matthew spent a lot of his free time at home, taking care of his twin sisters while his mom was teaching at a local community college. His parents were divorced, and he and his sisters stayed with their father every other weekend. Though no one else said it out loud, it was apparent that money was tight for them.

My heart squeezed. Our family never worried about money. We weren't crazy rich or anything, but my parents had put us in after-school care when we were younger without a second thought.

I nibbled at my lasagna and stole peeks around his house. Small knickknacks scattered across the windowsill, which was open to let in the early evening sun. The table and chairs were solid wood and a little scuffed, but clean and polished. I liked the house a lot—it was inviting, friendly. It made me want to sit down and make myself comfortable.

My house was much different. Mom had art everywhere, pieces she'd collected during big vacations with Dad. Our furniture wasn't plush, but more sleek and modern. Muted colors and contemporary style. Sparse furnishing to make the big rooms look even bigger. Not like this place.

We usually only ate dinner together once or twice a week, which was why I was just gonna grab something out of the freezer and heat it up after my meeting with Matthew. This was definitely better than frozen pizza.

Suddenly I realized everyone was looking at me. I paused midbite. Had they asked me a question I'd missed because of looking around and getting lost in my own thoughts? "Um," I stalled.

"Mom wanted to know how you're liking the art class so far," Matthew said with a knowing smile.

"Oh, it's great." I talked a bit about the pieces we'd worked on so far. "There are a lot of talented people in there. It's challenging and fun."

Matthew's mom beamed at him. "Matt worked so hard to get in. He was the only full scholarship recipient for the program. He's an amazing artist—as I'm sure you've seen already."

I couldn't help but smile, especially as he squirmed in his seat. "That's awesome." I also couldn't help the small twinge of jealousy in my chest, watching the love pouring from his mom's eyes. Yes, my parents supported me. But they'd never gushed about my art like this. For them, this was a side project, something that distracted me before school started.

When the summer was over, it was expected that I'd pick my regular routine back up and art would be on the back burner. My life would revolve around nonstop academics again. Once, I would have been excited for the challenge. Now I was kinda dreading it.

"How long have you been doing art?" I asked, curious to learn more about Matthew.

He swiped at an errant lock of hair that had fallen across his forehead, and my fingers itched to touch it. "Um, forever?" He gave a self-conscious laugh.

"Mom said Matthew used to paint with everything, all over the walls," Carmen said, shoveling food into her mouth. "Pizza sauce. Crayons. Pancake batter. She grounded him when he was little for using her nail polish all over the mirror."

"In my defense, it was a self-portrait," he said, rolling his eyes. "And the brush was small enough for detail work."

His mom snorted. "You're lucky you're cute, Matthew."

Boy, was she right about that. When he smiled, that dimple popped out and drew my eyes like a magnet.

It was fun and interesting to see him around his family. He didn't seem so self-assured, the way he came across in school or even in our art class. He was strangely . . . vulnerable, like he was afraid of me judging him. If only he knew that that sweetness made me soften up even more.

I dragged my attention to my plate and made myself focus on eating instead of staring at him so much. Good thing the lasagna was so tasty. It helped provide a solid distraction from my thoughts.

Matthew and his family talked as dinner went on. I quietly watched their dynamic. He was fun but firm with his sisters, nudging them to lower their voices when they got too excited or loud. They respected him without questioning it, which made me think he'd probably been helping his mom take care of them for a while.

His mom was right—there was plenty of food to be had. I found myself finishing my plate and getting seconds, something I normally didn't do at other people's houses. But she was a great cook.

When we finished, my belly full, she grabbed the plates. I stood to help.

"Oh, no, you're a guest here." She eyed the twins, who grudgingly got out of their seats to help her clear.

Leaving me alone with Matthew.

"So, that's my family," he said with a chuckle, eyes flashing with the low laugh. "They're loud and crazy."

"I really like them." I poured earnestness into my tone. "They seem like they care about you a lot." I knew my family cared, but we didn't do the little things like his did. His mom reaching over to pat his back as she bragged about his art. The way his sisters bragged about his talents. Yup, that little flare of envy got a smidge bigger. Our family wasn't much on displays of emotion, public or private. But I hadn't realized I really wanted it until now.

"It's been just the four of us for a while. We're all pretty close." Matthew stood and peeked into the kitchen. "Need any help?"

"I'm good," his mom hollered. "Go, have fun." She stepped out and wiped her hands quickly on a dish towel, then reached over and hugged me. "It was nice meeting you. I hope you'll come back over again soon. You're welcome anytime!"

She genuinely meant it—I could tell by the warm smile creasing her face. "Thanks again for dinner. It was great."

She shooed us out the door. "And next time you come, I'll show you all of Matthew's baby pictures."

He groaned and tried to push me out faster.

I laughed and threw out over my shoulder, "It's a date!"

The sun was descending toward the horizon as we made our way back to the park. It was empty now, quiet, with only small gusts of warm breezes flowing. Funny how one impulsive decision had changed things. I was seeing Matthew in a slightly different light, getting more and more information about his character. Every time I was around him, the mental portrait I had of him got another wash of color.

We headed to the middle of the park, where there was a set of swings. Matthew plopped down in one, and I took the seat beside him. I kicked off my sandals and ran my toes through the still-warm sand beneath my feet.

"So, now you've learned all this embarrassing stuff about me," he said. "Your turn to be in the hot spot. Tell me about you. And it had better be good."

I stuck out my tongue. "I'm boring. I never painted on walls." I kicked my feet and began to swing. Air rushed around me. I leaned back in my seat, gripping the metal chains, and straightened my whole body out. The sky moved back and forth above me, the last remains of sunlight dappling through the trees. When was the last time I'd just relaxed like this? "I work too hard," I blurted out, surprised to realize I meant it.

My constant need to be the best at everything meant I worked,

worked, worked all the time. Free time was more time to study, to keep aiming for number one. Which meant I missed out on these quieter moments. Funny how I didn't realize how much I craved it until right now. With him.

"Why do you push yourself so hard?" he asked. "What is it you're aiming for?"

I pointed my toes and kept my attention on the sky. I wasn't sure I was ready to really spill my deepest feelings. There was something scary about being so vulnerable with a person . . . especially one I was growing increasingly attracted to. "Oh, well, I just love to win," I said with a laugh. "And speaking of, we need to talk about our project."

My diversion worked. "Are you struggling half as much as I am?" he asked. "I just can't seem to get in the groove of it. I'm not feeling it the way I should be."

I slowed my swing and sat up to look at him. "Me too. I've never had a piece frustrate me as much as this one does. I keep working on it but it isn't getting any better. Do you still think it's the right one for us?"

The light danced along the top of his head, making him glow. I couldn't stop staring. My heart rate picked up again, and I swallowed. It was getting harder to fight these feelings, despite all my efforts. *We're really different,* I kept telling myself. We'd never work out. And then I'd end up hurt and brokenhearted. I just couldn't risk it.

Matthew shrugged. "Honestly? I don't know. But we may need to go back to the drawing board."

I groaned. It had taken us so long to get here.

"Or maybe we just need some fresh inspiration to help us inject new life into the project." He stopped swinging, stood, and grabbed my hand. "Come on. Let's find it. You have your phone, right?"

His hand was firm, wrapped around mine, as he tugged me out of the swing. I barely had time to grab my shoes, laughing. "Hold on, hold on," I said as I slipped into them, then dug my phone out with my free hand. "Okay, I'm ready."

We ran to the sidewalk that edged the park and began to stroll, still holding hands. I was so nervous that I was afraid he'd feel my fingers shaking, my palms sweating. But he held my hand like it was something we did every day. Like we were friends. Did it mean anything to him?

Matthew tugged his phone out of his pocket with his free hand. He stopped me and turned me to face him. My arms tingled from the light pressure of his hands on my skin. I struggled to keep my breathing even and pretend like everything was cool.

"Okay," he said. "I have an idea. Go take pictures of five things that surprise you. Whoever finds the best shot will get to tell the other how we should fix our art project. And maybe we can even use some element of what we took a picture of. Sound fair?"

A strange challenge, but my pulse picked up in excitement. Just the challenge I needed. I was going to win this for sure. "How will we know which one is the best?" I said with a crooked grin.

"I think we'll know. I trust us to be unbiased." He leaned

close to me, and his mouth was just a few inches away. His eyes glanced down at my lips, then darted back to my eyes. "Do you?"

I swallowed, nodded. My heart fluttered like a trapped bird. All I could smell was his skin, the gentle scent of his cologne. He wrapped around me like a summer morning, and I wanted to lean in, breathe deeply.

He leaned back, breaking the spell. I blinked and made myself shake off the moment. Obviously it was just in my head.

"Fine. Meet back here in fifteen minutes," I said, then turned and walked off without looking back.

Good grief. I bit the inside of my cheek for a welcome, painful flash of reality. *Stop being so dumb,* I chastised myself. *You're partners. That's it. You can't keep going around, thinking about how good he smells or how big and warm his hands are. Knock it off.*

The voice in my head jarred me enough to help me turn my attention back to our challenge.

I scoured the ground, the air, the trees. I made myself look at everything with a new, fresh eye. What surprised me? The sun was descending fast, taking with it the last of the day's light. I was running out of time to get good shots.

I saw a piece of paper skittering across the sidewalk. On it were a bunch of crossed-out hearts, hand drawn in pencil. Well, that was interesting. I took a shot.

One down, four to go.

From there, once I opened myself up to take everything in, I found the rest of my pictures. There was a patch of grass shaped like a question mark. An old tennis shoe with the back heel cut off. A spot on a tree that had been carved with the words "I exist."

Just one more picture to find.

I turned around and saw the long length of my shadow—the tip of it, my head, was resting on the tree trunk. It was cool and weird, so I took the picture and dashed back to meet Matthew. What images had he found, and would he find mine interesting, the way I had? My lungs tightened in anticipation.

Right on the dot, Matthew strolled back toward me. The sky was aflame with pinks and purples as dusk pulled across the horizon. Streetlights around the park and sidewalks flickered on and hummed to life. It was quiet and intimate with no one else around, like the park belonged to just us.

Crud. Mom would expect me home soon. But I didn't want to go, not yet. I could hang out a few more minutes, at least.

"What did you find?" he asked me as he neared. We walked over to a bench and sat down. His thigh bounced lightly beside mine, our jeans rubbing just a touch.

I gave him my phone and tried to stay cool as he flicked through my images, one at a time. Slowly. He took a moment to really digest each one.

"Wow." His face was dead serious, and he had a look of appreciation in his eyes. "I really like those. You have an interesting eye for composition." He flicked back to the image of the paper. "This one is funny and sad at the same time. Why would someone make all that effort to draw hearts and then cross them out? I wonder about that person's story. This picture *makes* me wonder about it."

I flushed from the unexpected compliment. Somehow, hearing him praise my art made me feel like a real artist. "Thanks, Matthew. This was an interesting idea. Now let me see yours."

He clicked to the camera roll and handed me his phone. I couldn't quite read his eyes, but the way he pursed his lips and bounced his leg more, it seemed like he was a little uneasy.

When I saw the first image, a laugh barked out of me. He'd taken his shoes off and had dug his heels into a small sandy patch. "Very cute," I said drolly.

"Hey, it surprised me how cool the sand was," he said with a laugh.

I kept going to the next image. A far-off shot all the way across the park of an old man and woman holding hands as they walked a tiny fluffy white dog—they had to be well in their eighties, bodies hunched over, love pouring from their wrinkled smiles. I swallowed, a lump growing in my chest. The image was potent with emotion and stole my breath.

The next image was a broken plastic bracelet, discarded by the sidewalk. The fourth was a pair of raggedy pants with rips on the knees, laid evenly out on the grass.

"Someone's probably gonna get cold tonight," I said with a chuckle.

I looked at the last image, and the air sucked from my lungs. It was a close-up shot of my face, me biting my lower lip as I studied my shadow on the tree. The sun glinted off my cheeks, illuminating my skin to a dusky, warm brown. My lashes fluttered along the tops of my cheeks. In that moment I looked . . . intense.

Beautiful.

No one had ever taken a picture like that of me before.

I glanced up at him, the phone gripped tightly in my hand. "Why did you— What—" I had no words. I was flustered.

His gaze skittered away. "*You* surprise me," he said simply.

I surprised him. *Me.* The girl who loved math and competition. The one who had snubbed him and his style of art until he'd started forcing me to open my eyes to the world around me.

Matthew was feeling this . . . thing . . . between us too. A prospect that simultaneously thrilled and scared me to the core.

Chapter ☻ Thirteen

think I'm the winner," he said in a quiet tone. It wasn't gloating, though.

I still wasn't sure how to respond. I handed him back his phone. "Hm. Maybe you are." Even without the picture of me, he'd gotten some interesting images. "So what does this mean?"

"I have some ideas." He looked up at the sky and grimaced. "I have to be heading home soon though, before the twins make my mom go crazy. If you have time, can we talk about it more after class tomorrow?"

"Sure." I straightened my back and tried to shake off the weird, unsettling euphoria that had settled in my chest. I didn't want to go. I wanted to stand right here, suspended in time, in the warm glow of a summer dusk with this guy. He surprised me, made me laugh.

Stole my breath away.

"Let me walk you home," he said.

"Oh, I'm fine. Really."

He raised an eyebrow. "My mom would kill me if I didn't escort you."

That euphoric feeling sank just a bit. So he was doing it out of a sense of duty. I swallowed back my disappointment. "Fine."

It was a little over a mile to my house. The first chunk was walked in quiet. The street was pretty quiet, with only the occasional car zipping by.

"Why do you like to win so much?" Matthew asked, breaking the awkward silence between us.

"Don't you like to win?" I fired back. After all, he was in this competition with me. Plus, he played basketball, and sports thrived on the art of winning.

His steps were quiet beside me. Cicadas and crickets chirped in the grasses and trees around us. "Sure I do. But I kinda get the feeling you like it more than the average person."

Maybe so. Winning was how I felt special. It gave me tangible goals, evidence that I could succeed at whatever I wanted to.

It made people respect me. It made my parents notice me.

The realization squeezed my throat, and I dragged in a quiet breath, trying not to give away the rush of emotion. "I . . . need to be good at the things I do," I admitted. "I just happen to do a lot of things."

"You seem to be a bit of an overachiever." The words were soft, but they might as well have been a slap across my face.

So that was how he viewed me? In such a negative light? The word "overachiever" wasn't a compliment. It meant someone who was a workaholic, like my parents. I sped up my pace, my feet clipping along the sidewalk.

"Hey," he said, darting back up to my side. "What's the deal?"

I froze in place, and he stopped a split second after me. I planted my hands on my hips. "Why is wanting to win a bad thing? I set goals, and I go after what I want. But you know what? I don't need to rationalize any of that to you." Who was he to judge me, anyway?

A tiny thought niggled at the back of my mind. *You judged him first*, it declared, despite my efforts to ignore it. But this was different. This was below the belt, hitting me in a particularly sensitive spot.

"I'm fine to walk home alone," I continued, proud of the way my voice didn't wobble with all of my emotions. "I'll see you tomorrow in class." With that, I spun and walked away from him. My face burned with frustration, irritation, mixed with a healthy dose of mortification.

When I reached our front door, I tossed it open and ran right up for my bedroom, offering a mumbled hello to my parents, who were sitting on the couch. I closed my door behind me and plopped down on my bed.

It took me a good ten minutes to finally shake off my immediate feelings of frustration. And once I did, guilt edged in. It wasn't

Matthew's fault I was oversensitive about the topic, torn between wanting to please my parents and wanting to be my own person. He was still getting to know me. No way could he have realized it was one of my personal triggers.

In fact, after replaying it in my head again—this time with a more unbiased perspective—his comment hadn't even been that harsh.

I bit my lip, remembering the picture he'd taken of me. How I'd almost looked ethereal. Was that how he saw me? Yes, he'd called me an overachiever. But had he been wrong in that? He was just being honest.

It was painfully clear now, upon thinking things over with a clear head, that I'd overreacted.

I swiped a hand across my face. I'd judged him without question or hesitation when we'd first met. I'd thought he was a dumb jock, and he'd proven me wrong time and again. He was sensitive, smart, witty. Had he really been judging me out there, or was he just commenting on something that was a fact?

I'd gotten hotheaded and walked away, letting my emotions run rampant. Who was the bigger jerk here?

I dug out my phone and stared at it. Should I call? Text? I started and erased several messages. Nothing seemed to say what I wanted to say. Maybe it would be better to talk in person tomorrow, when he could see my face.

Plus, to be honest, I needed to shake him off for a bit. The fact that I reacted so strongly to his words, had assumed the worst, disturbed me just as much as the words had themselves. He was getting under my skin beyond just a stupid crush. The realization freaked me out and made me want more all at the same time.

I needed time with my best friend. I jumped to my desk and opened my laptop, firing up my messenger.

FoxyCori: U up? I know it's late, lol.

I glanced at the computer and did the mental math. Scotland was five hours ahead of us, so it was almost two in the morning. Odds were, Ava was probably unconscious right now.

FoxyCori: Msg me in AM? I'll be up at 6 (11 ur time). Just want to say hi!

With that, I closed down my computer and set about my evening. The routine of shower, brushing teeth, and reading was soothing, though it didn't diminish my angst. What was Matthew doing right now? Was he mad at me?

By ten, I was ready to call it a night, especially if I hoped to talk to Ava in the morning. But it took me quite a while to actually fall asleep. My guilty conscience kept me awake long into the night. I couldn't get Matthew's hurt face out of my mind.

AvaBee: Im here! You awake?

AvaBee: Scotland is so foggy so far, lol.

FoxyCori: Hey, yes, Im awake! Kinda. ;-)

I rubbed sleep out of my eyes. The room had an early morning glow, with soft light pouring through my window.

A photograph of rolling fog over a scraggly, grassy field,

complete with several roaming sheep, popped up as a link on the messenger screen. The green stretched as far as the eye could see. It was gorgeous; I could almost smell the damp-tinged air.

AvaBee: Mom and Dad r getting ready. Going to tour castles 2day. How are you?

I sighed, wondering what I should type. I didn't want to be a downer. While I ached to unload all of my frustration on Ava's shoulders, I also didn't need to be *that* person.

FoxyCori: Oh, not bad. Class in a couple of hrs.

AvaBee: Almost convincing. LOL. Wassup? Tell me or I'll be forced 2 make somethin up in my head.

She always could see through me. I laughed quietly under my breath. In a few sentences I summed up what had happened yesterday, including the picture and the argument.

AvaBee: Wow. I think he likes you a lot.

I blinked. Not the response I'd been expecting from her. A warm flush stole across my cheeks as I thought of his smile. Then the guilty turbulence came back in my stomach. We were partners. I needed to stop daydreaming about him. Besides, he was probably mad about the way I'd stomped off.

FoxyCori: Hard to tell. Sometimes I think so. Other times he plays it cool.

AvaBee: I keep telling u that u shld give it a chance. He's nice.

FoxyCori: *shrug* We'll see. Take tons of pics! And find a cute bf while you're there.

AvaBee: *blush* There is this v cute guy in our hotel . . .

FoxyCori: MORE DETAILS PLS

I laughed. Leave it to Ava to be in Scotland and already attract a guy. She was a magnetic person, though, so I had no doubt that by the end of the trip, the guy would be begging for her to stay in touch.

We spent the next twenty minutes just chatting about Scotland, her mysterious cute guy—who apparently was British with a "darling accent," as she put it—and how many castles she wanted to buy. I was relieved to have the focus of the conversation off me and my drama. As much as it had felt good to spill it all out at the time, it had also made my flare-up of guilt return with a vengeance.

I needed to talk to Matthew and sort this out, not run from it and let my hot head rule. There was no way we could work together with this between us. And I had to admit, I didn't like the idea of him being upset with me. Part of me wanted him to see me as more than just an overachiever.

I ended the conversation with Ava and set out my clothes, then took a quick shower. I took a little bit of extra care with my makeup and then my hair, twisting it into small spiraling braids. Then I headed downstairs.

Charlie was stuffing cereal into his face. Dad was at the table, sipping coffee, and Mom was washing her coffee mug.

"Oh, hey, honey," she said. She raised an eyebrow as she eyed me. "You're looking very cute today."

I gave a casual shrug and poured a glass of juice. My stomach was too nervous to eat anything—I took small sips and hoped she'd drop the subject.

"How's your project going?" Dad asked as he grabbed a section of the newspaper. "You and that boy figure out what you're going to do?"

I gave a weak nod, hoping the wobbly smile on my face appeared genuine.

Dad looked up, and a deep line furrowed his brow. "What's wrong?"

Dang. He always could read me too easily. I was afraid to let them know about the argument or how badly our project was going. Because if I heard *you should have just stuck with focusing on academics* from them, it was going to crush me.

I kept seeing Matthew's mom's face, full of pride as she gushed about his art. I craved seeing that look on my parents' faces too. All the more reason why I needed to win this competition. They could see how talented I was in something other than schoolwork and be proud of me.

"Nothing's wrong," I made myself say. "I . . . got up early to talk to Ava, so I'm just a little sleepy."

He eyed me for a moment, then grunted, sipping his coffee. "I hope she's having fun. But you gotta get more sleep, Corinne. Try to plan out your conversations better with her in the future."

I nodded and finished the last of my juice. Mom took the glass from my hand before I could rinse it myself. "I gotta run to class." Time to man up and face Matthew.

My stomach lurched. No, it was going to be fine. He was a reasonable guy—and if he held a grudge even after I apologized for my rash reaction, then that was his problem, not mine. *So stop stressing about it,* I ordered myself.

Still, my heart raced the entire way to the studio.

Chapter Fourteen

showed up at class right before it was supposed to start. Matthew wasn't there. My lungs squeezed in disappointment and relief.

Then worry.

He was always here on time—was he going to cut class because he was upset with me? I grabbed my tub of paint and started putting out my shades on the palette. But my hand was trembling, and I got a few splotches on the table.

"You okay?" Henry asked as he studied me. "You seem . . . a little off today."

I nodded and wiped the paint clean. "Oh, yeah, I'm just a little distracted."

Teni wandered up the aisle to look at our progress. She stood behind me and Henry. His image was a house in shades of purple—it was creepy, like something in a Victorian nightmare. "Henry, this is great. I love the vibe in the image. Dark, gothic. Very nice mood. Make sure you remember how paint texture can also add to the scene. Don't be afraid to show your paint strokes."

He beamed, pleased by her compliment. "Thanks, and good idea." He started dabbing at an almost-black window, and the thick clump made it look like there was a shadow lurking behind a curtain.

"Corinne, this is coming along well." She pointed at my red painting in progress of the lake at sunset. "Very interesting subject matter. What made you choose red to paint it? Most people would have gone with blue or green."

I pointed at the sunset, where red poured in streams from the setting sun. "It felt like going with reds and pinks was better for a sunset. And the color gives it more warmth than you'd get from blue or green."

She nodded. "Looking great. Don't be afraid to loosen up those lines. Red is a passionate color. Pull that emotion out from your heart and be free with it. Don't hold yourself back."

She walked off, and I stared at my painting. How could I unleash that emotion? Passion—I felt it, for sure. It sparked under my skin when I thought of art. But it never quite seemed to translate to the paper the way I wanted it to.

What could I do to push it to the next level?

A soft whisper brushed against my ear, and instantly my skin tingled with awareness. "Can we talk after class?" It was Matthew, peering down at me. He looked tired, his hair disheveled. His brow was furrowed. But there was no anger in his eyes. Just a touch of wariness.

I gave a wordless nod, drinking him in.

He nodded in return and then proceeded to his station, squirting dollops of green onto his pallet. I watched him use a pallet knife to get a thick scoop up and streak it down the canvas. I couldn't tell what his scene was yet since he was focusing on layering in all the dark shades first, but it intrigued me.

Class passed painfully slowly, minutes ticking by in a drag. I was distracted by the lingering scent of Matthew's skin, how his words had brushed against my ear, the emotions in his eyes. What did he want to say to me?

Finally, Teni told us it was time to wrap up. I rinsed off my palette and brushes and cleaned up my station. Students filed out into the bright afternoon sunshine. I lingered at my table, waiting for Matthew to finish his work. By now, my stomach was a mass of wild butterflies.

When he was done, he turned to me and indicated with his head that we should go outside. I followed him through the door into the heat. The afternoon sun had kicked in—it had to be in the nineties outside right now.

Sweat trickled down my back. "Can we go over there?" I asked, pointing toward a large shade tree a few feet away.

He nodded, and we sat down at the base of the trunk. It wasn't much cooler, but at least the sun wasn't scorching us.

"Hey—" he started, right as I said, "Um—"

We both paused and gave self-conscious laughs.

Matthew raked his hand through his hair. "I'm sorry for making you so mad last night." His voice was low, rumbling. "I didn't mean it as an insult, but I can see why you took it that way. I hope you're not still angry with me."

I swallowed. "No, I'm sorry. I was unfair to walk away like that without even talking." I paused, swallowed again. More sweat dribbled down my torso, and I fanned my neckline to get air flowing against my skin. "I'm a little oversensitive about it."

His gaze danced across the horizon as he watched people walk by on the sidewalk. "I didn't mean to push. I'm just curious about you. You seem like you can do everything, like you're good at everything. It makes me want to know what makes you happy."

His words made me pause. What did make me happy? Being good at academics gave me a sense of pride, accomplishment. But did it fill me with joy? The rush I got from success never seemed to last long enough. I was always chasing that next rush, hoping it would give me that feeling again.

The realization made me a little sad. What else did I have if I wasn't winning, being the best? Was my life nothing more than a string of accomplishments, checked off on some never-ending mental list?

"I think art makes me genuinely happy," I finally said. "But it also challenges me because it's not something measurable. Instead, its measurement comes from enjoyment."

"I think we need to try something else," Matthew blurted.

"What?"

"For our project. This isn't the right one." He leaned toward me, peered down into my eyes. My skin tingled in response to the intense stare. "We both know it—we need to scrap it and start over. I've wanted to talk to you about it for a couple of days now but I just didn't know how."

He was right. Our project wasn't flowing. It was missing something—that sense of enjoyment, for starters.

I gave a slow nod. "Okay. Do you have any ideas?"

The weight seemed to disappear off his shoulders. His whole being lightened, and it was like having the intensity of the sun on me full force. I couldn't help but get warmer. "I do. I know time is running out, but I got an idea last night and I think it would work out great."

My lungs froze in anticipation. For some reason, I knew whatever he was going to say would be important.

"We need to paint each other. Split the screen as we did before, but we paint half of the face of the other person—the way we see each other. Honestly. So we can still use the split-image idea we both agreed on, but with better subjects. Ourselves."

I blinked, scrubbed a hand across my face, trying to wrap my mind around it. Our faces blending together. Him drawing the lines of my eyes.

My mouth.

A lump grew in my throat. Oh man, that meant we'd be

spending hours staring at each other while we composed our halves of the image. It was going to be intense and emotional. Was I ready for it?

But I had to admit, it was a good idea. A great one, even. And if we could pull it off . . . it could be intriguing enough to help us win.

I straightened my back as a breeze whipped around the tree, fluttering the hem of my shirt. Matthew and I had to go big with this one. We had to make it just right. So I would push aside my self-consciousness and take a risk.

Just like Teni had advised us to.

"Okay," I said softly. "I'm in. Let's give this idea of yours a try."

We went back inside to catch Teni before she left, explaining the idea and asking if we could use the studio on Saturday, after I was done working at the bakery. She tilted her head and listened as Matthew explained his vision.

"I like it," she declared, looking at me. "It will be interesting to see how Matthew portrays you in a modern style, Corinne. And how you'll bring your classical art style into his design. It's intriguing and personal." She beamed at us. "Yes, come on Saturday. Time is running out, so make sure to let me know if you two need anything else."

After we left the studio, I went to turn toward my house, but Matthew caught my hand.

"We good?" he asked, and there was a thread of something in his voice that made the breath hitch in my throat.

I could only nod.

His thumb caressed the flesh of my palm as he squeezed my hand and walked away. I watched him go, heart slamming in my chest, hand almost on fire from the soft scorch of his touch.

I anticipated Saturday and feared it like nothing I'd ever experienced before. But I had a feeling it was going to be one intense day.

I floated all the way back home.

Matthew slid his hand along my arm, making the flesh erupt in a million goose bumps. "Right here, please," he said. He was totally in artist mode, not seeing me as Corinne but as the subject of his piece.

I only wished I could maintain such professionalism right now. I could barely make my lungs function with him this close.

For the last few minutes, Matthew had been posing me, playing with the blinds to determine how much light he wanted on my face. Shifting my body to just the right angle. Doing everything a savvy artist does to prepare the subject.

I, on the other hand, had been awkward and gawky. Matthew had met me here at the studio after I'd gotten off work, saying he wanted to work on me first. I'd never been a model before, so this was all new to me.

"Perfect," he declared, stepping back.

It was Saturday afternoon, and I was seated on a stool at the front of Teni's studio. The shades had been lifted so light indirectly shone on my skin. At least I wouldn't be sweating in front of him—that would be far too embarrassing.

I'd taken a lot of care with my appearance today, knowing he was going to be staring intently at me. My makeup was soft and subtle, just enough to highlight my cheekbones and the curve of my lower lip. A little bit of mascara to make my lashes seem longer and thicker. Charlie had laughed at me for spending so long in the bathroom—I'd shoved him out and locked the door behind me.

It was worth the effort and time to look my best. For the painting, of course, I told myself.

"Okay, stay still. I'm going to do some sketches of you." Matthew had a tone that said he was completely in control. He'd definitely shifted into artist mode.

We were silent for the first twenty minutes or so. The clock was on the far wall behind him so at least I was able to see how much time was passing. I kept my gaze forward, trying not to look at Matthew. Knowing he was staring at my skin, seeing all the blemishes and flaws. How one of my ears was slightly higher than the other.

"Relax your face," he said with a grin. "Your mouth just thinned into a tight line. Are you okay?"

"I'm just nervous," I admitted. "I've never done this before." I rubbed my damp palms on my shorts-clad thighs.

He tapped his chin with the bottom of his pencil as he stared at his easel. I couldn't see what he was drawing, only the back of the paper. "Where is your favorite vacation spot?"

I froze in place. "Huh?" The question came out of left field.

He turned those brilliant blue eyes to me, and a slow smile crawled across his face. "Mine is the Grand Canyon. You never realize how small people are until you see something so massive in comparison. It was amazing. I've always wanted to try to capture it in a drawing somehow, but I don't know how to show the sheer scale of it."

I closed my eyes for a second as I ran through my mental memory bank. Our family used to go on vacations back when I was a kid, though since Mom and Dad were working more now, that didn't happen as much. But I still remembered one that made me smile. "As corny as it sounds, one of our best trips was to Disneyland."

I heard his pencil scratching on the paper. "What made it so great?"

"Well, it was more the fact that we were all together, just relaxing. We saw some shows, ate a lot of food, laughed the entire time." I smiled, still remembering vivid flashes of the vacation. The air had been warm. Brilliant fireworks exploding at night. We'd stuffed our faces with cotton candy and junk food. Even Dad had relaxed his usual uptight self, holding Mom's hand as we'd all strolled down Main Street.

It sounded like Matthew's breath caught. I opened my eyes, but he was looking at the paper. Huh, I must have imagined it.

"What's your favorite food?" he asked me.

"Like I can pick one." I chuckled. "Um, I love mac and cheese. There's something so simple about it. You?"

"Chicken wings."

I raised an eyebrow. "Buffalo sauce or barbeque?"

He huffed. "Please. Buffalo sauce. Gimme the spicy all day long."

I leaned back slightly in the chair and crossed my feet at the ankles. I wasn't sure if it was his intention, but the conversation was helping me relax. I wasn't feeling so on the spot anymore.

"What is your biggest fear?" he asked me. He kept his attention on the drawing, his pencil making tiny skritching sounds.

I swallowed. I had lots of little fears—falling into a grate on the sidewalk, having a spider drop on my face, getting lost in a big city. But my biggest one so far linked deeply into the thing I prided myself on most.

My drive to succeed.

And yet, another ever-growing fear was edging its way to the forefront, something I had not anticipated happening. The fear of falling for Matthew and being utterly, devastatingly hurt if he didn't feel the same.

Or even worse, if he did, but we couldn't make a relationship work.

No way was I ready to admit to that to him, though. Falling for someone was like jumping off a cliff. I could see the cool, inviting water below and I knew it had the potential to be the most amazing thing I'd ever experienced. But that leap of faith, where you stuck your foot out over the edge and let yourself dive into the mysteries below the rippling surface . . . I wasn't ready for it yet.

The thought of giving in to the unknown petrified me.

But looking into Matthew's eyes, the color of the ocean, made an increasingly larger part of me want to abandon my fear and jump in headfirst.

Chapter ● Fifteen

I swallowed and turned my attention back to his question. "Um, I'm petrified of failure," I finally whispered. It was still a core fear, but safer than going down the other road . . . the one that involved him. "Not just losing competitions or being second place. It's something deeper, more painful than that. Failing at fulfilling my dreams. At not being good enough."

He paused his drawing and fixed those intense eyes on me. His nod was small but I could see his empathy. "I push myself hard on the basketball team. The more wins I get, the stronger I look. The stronger I look, the more likely important people will notice me. It might be the only way I can go to college someday—I need a scholarship."

Just like he needed the money from our competition. My

heart squeezed a bit. How hard it had to be to worry about money so much. I felt a flare of shame at how dismissive I was on the topic, how unappreciative I'd been of my easy life. I never had to worry about things being paid for. They simply were.

Judging by his posture, it didn't seem comfortable for him to drop his guard and tell me this vulnerability. But the fact that he did made me feel closer to him. The space between us narrowed, filled with unspoken words.

We sat in silence for a few more minutes. I could hear the soft huffs of his breath as he worked on my image, the sound of pencil on paper. The tick of the clock on the wall. What would it look like? How did he see me? I kept thinking about that picture he took of me in the park.

"Okay, I think I'm almost done," he said. After another minute or so, he put the pencil down and stopped. His eyes turned to me, and a nervous grin crawled across his face. "Now it's your turn."

I stood from the seat and stretched with a grimace as my back popped in a few spots. Wow, how did models do this for long sessions? Everything in my body was cramped and tight. "Get ready for the fun," I muttered. But my heart was racing in anticipation of seeing his drawing.

As I headed for him, he quickly covered his image. "Not ready yet," he said when I approached.

"Wait, what? I can't even take a peek? But we're working on it together." I looked up at him and saw a small smudge of pencil on his chin. Before I realized what I was doing, I reached my thumb up and swept it across the spot to clear it.

I froze, hand on skin. His eyes flared, and the breath hitched in his throat as his Adam's apple bobbed.

"Um." I swallowed, dropped my hand. "You had . . . there was a mark . . ." My face burned like it was a hundred degrees in the building.

Matthew moved in silence to the seat. I took my place behind the easel and prepared my station to draw.

There was a definite spark there between us, something that crackled like live electricity every time we got near. And when we touched, my skin felt like it was on fire. Scary and intoxicating—I was drawn to it and wanted to run at the same time.

Because I knew it meant big trouble.

I closed my eyes, drew in a slow breath. *Focus.* I needed to keep my attention on our work, where it belonged.

Matthew sat serenely staring over my shoulder, eyes fixed on the wall behind me. Good. It gave me space to pull myself together. I grabbed a pencil and began to rough out his outline. The way his hair tufted, the shell of his ears. The strong, firm angle of his jaw and the swoop of his lean throat.

My skin flushed as I took in all the details about him I hadn't let myself focus too much on before. How his nose had that tiny bump along the bridge. The series of freckles right at the V of his throat.

My fingers itched to stroke those spots and see if they were as warm as the rest of him was.

The pencil shook in my hand and I gripped it tighter. "Um." I cleared my throat again—it was starting to become a bad habit around him—and said, "Well, if you won't show me your picture, you have to wait for mine, too."

The corner of his lip curled up. "This is going to be interesting."

Slowly, as I worked, I slipped into the zone. I drew the way his hair flopped over his brow, captured the sparkle in his eyes from the light through the window. The dimple in his cheek. He was undeniably handsome, that was for sure. And while the girl in me was still nervous, the artist in me thrilled at the challenge of capturing him accurately.

Matthew stayed a lot more still than I had. He didn't squirm, just sat there in serene confidence.

As I started shading in certain spots, I found myself wanting to ask him more questions about himself. Had he ever had a girlfriend?

Or been in love?

"Do you like school?" I blurted out and instantly wished I could smack my forehead. Wow, could I sound any nerdier?

The dimple flared in his cheek. "School is okay. I don't hate it." He shrugged. "My friends help me pass the time in boring classes."

"What classes *do* you like?"

He blinked. "Um, history is cool. I'm looking forward to physics next year. I really like science."

Never would have pegged him for a science guy. "I really like math, especially geometry."

He gave a knowing nod. "I should have assumed as much."

"Why do you say that?"

"Well," he started slowly, "you're drawn to classical art. You like rules. There's a sort of math in the art of perspective, shading, and so on. Math may seem stuffy, but it has a lot of applicable functions in life. Even in art."

I hadn't thought about it before, but he was right. The two did feed into each other. Maybe my interests weren't so polarized after all.

"Are you getting close to finishing?" he asked with a chuckle. "This chair isn't exactly the most comfortable, as you already know."

"Oh. Yeah." I could have sat here all day, staring at his face and drawing his likeness on paper. But that wasn't practical. Not to mention it would make me look super creepy. On impulse, I dug my phone out of my pocket and stepped a little closer to him. "But I'd like to take some shots of you. You know, so I can work on this more at home."

Not a total lie—I did want to keep going with this, and having his image would help. But more than that, I wanted to be able to look at him when he wasn't around.

Wow, I was falling *so* deep. I could see myself careening toward the edge of that cliff already. *Danger!* my brain tried to yell at me, but I couldn't seem to back away from the edge.

He lifted his chin up just a fraction so I got a better shot of his face in the light. "Okay, have at it."

I took several from different angles. The last one was straight on. His eyes roared to life, a sea of blue. My heart raced as I made myself close my phone and tuck it back into my pocket. "Um, I think I'm all done here."

He grabbed his phone, rotated me until I was facing the clock wall, and snapped a couple of shots of me, too.

"Hey, you already had one of my face," I said, knowing my cheeks were probably flaring red right now.

"But not in this particular location," he pointed out. "Need to make sure our light sources match for our project."

Duh. My heart sank a bit. Of course—he was thinking about shading and light for when we weren't in the studio.

I felt like a fool.

I put away my supplies in silence, and he did the same. We turned off the lights and exited the studio, locking the door behind us—Teni would be coming by soon to work on her own art.

I shifted my bag on my shoulder, my big art notebook clutched in my sweaty palm. "Okay, I'll see you on Monday," I said. I turned to walk down the street.

He touched my arm, wrapped his fingers around my skin. I froze in place and turned to face him. "What's wrong?" he asked.

"With me?" I shrugged casually and gave a wide smile. "Oh, nothing." Except that I was a total idiot who wouldn't stop reading into everything Matthew did, hoping somehow it would help me see how he was feeling about me. Wondering if this fire in my belly was matched by one in his.

I was totally becoming *that* girl.

He looked at me for a long moment, his eyes flaring with a bit of skepticism. But apparently he decided not to push. He released my arm. "Okay. I'll see you, then."

I stiffened my spine, pride flooding me. I wasn't going to let him know how I was feeling, how vulnerable I'd been in there. The project. That was my focus, my drive.

And as I walked back to my house, I almost managed to convince myself of it.

"Grandpa, can you pass me the gravy?" Charlie thrust out his hand across the table.

Mom shot him a glare.

Charlie huffed out a "please."

Grandpa handed him the bowl. "He's got your attitude," he told my mom, laughter in his wizened eyes. "You were a feisty one as a kid."

Sunday dinner was always like this—a little bit of teasing and a lot of food. Today was no different. Our table was heaped with fluffy biscuits and sausage gravy, thick slices of bacon, hot stacks of pancakes. Sometimes Mom liked to make breakfast for dinner, and I never protested because it was so good.

Dad buttered a biscuit. "Corinne, how's your art project

going? You've been holed up in your room a lot over the last couple of weeks."

I poured syrup on my pancakes and took a bite before answering, letting the maple fill my mouth. "Not bad. We were working on something but decided to try another route, since it just wasn't flowing."

This afternoon, I'd gone to a drugstore and had them print a copy of Matthew's picture out so I could use it for reference for my painting. It was in my room right now, taped on the wall by my easel. His eyes looked endless, like they saw right through me—the picture had taken my breath away when I saw it enlarged.

My cheeks burned at the thought. Even the drug store employee had commented on what a great shot it was.

"Why are you blushing?" Charlie asked in a loud voice.

I shot him a glare, willing my face to even out. The last thing I needed was for Mom and Dad to realize I had a crush on my art partner. They'd never let me live it down.

Dad furrowed his brow as he stared at me. I tilted my chin up and tried not to look intimidated. "You're still keeping up on your studies, aren't you?" he asked, a thin layer of disapproval in his voice.

Truthfully, I hadn't opened my math book in days. I'd been busy with art, letting it consume my world, my thoughts.

Art, and Matthew.

I cleared my throat. "Math stuff is still going fine." It wasn't like math theories were suddenly going to change or anything.

But I knew better than to say that to my dad, who would see it as mouthing off.

Grandpa raised an eyebrow. "And how is it, working with that boy? Matthew, is that his name? Are you guys getting along okay?"

I nodded. "We figured out a project that melds both of our artistic styles. I think we have a real chance." All I knew was that I had a lot of excitement at the thought of painting his face. I was ready to pour all of my passion into it. I needed this to be my best project ever.

Mom finished the last bite of biscuit on her plate. Then she said, "You guys have been spending an awful lot of time together lately." There was a thread of discomfort in her tone.

My heart rate picked up. "We have to—we're getting close to the deadline."

"When it's done, I expect to see you returning your focus back to your schoolwork," Dad said. "Classes will be starting again soon, and you don't want to get behind."

A swell of frustration filled me. Ava was off in Scotland, enjoying a wonderful family vacation with her parents. Meanwhile, mine were trying to keep my nose stuck in a book all summer, not outside enjoying the weather. Art. Life, really.

"I'm not going to get behind." I knew my voice had a snippy tone but I couldn't help it. I was tired of being pushed so hard. I liked math—loved it. But couldn't I love it on my own terms? Did it have to be everything, all the time?

The table got quiet. Even my brother turned his attention to his plate, like he knew there was a fight brewing.

I stood and grabbed my half-eaten plate. "I'm going to go upstairs and work." I didn't want to argue. I just wanted to get back into that happy glowing place I experienced every time I lost myself in art.

Mom gave me a short nod. I didn't even look at my father or anyone else as I headed to the kitchen, emptied my plate, and dumped it in the sink. Then I made my way into my bedroom, trying to fight the sting of tears.

I dug the heels of my hands into my eyes. No, I wasn't going to cry. Not over this. I just had to find a way to make them understand that art was just as important to me as schoolwork.

I needed the freedom to explore both. But if Dad had his way, that was not going to happen.

My gaze turned to Matthew's image. The soft glow of light on his skin. The flare in his eyes. I studied my rough drawing beside it. Then I picked up my pencil and let myself get lost in the picture.

I didn't know how much time had passed until a soft knock on my bedroom door jarred me out of my zone. I put my pencil down. "Come in."

The door cracked open, and my grandpa's head stuck through the gap. He gave me a tentative smile and then came inside. When he saw my drawing, he stopped, stared at it for a long moment.

My breath caught in my lungs. What would he think of it?

"This is truly your best work," he finally said. "I see your heart in this piece already, even at sketch form. You have feelings for this boy, don't you."

I gave a miserable nod. "Been trying to fight it, but they're there."

Grandpa gave me a sympathetic smile and patted my shoulder. "Your father just wants what's best for you. Don't get discouraged. Stay true to yourself."

I nodded.

He gave me a quick hug and opened the door. As he went to leave, Mom came inside. She stood right in the doorway for a moment, arms crossed over her chest.

"Corinne," she said, her voice heavy. "We need to talk."

Chapter ● Sixteen

y lungs squeezed tight, but I kept my face as neutral as possible. "Yes, I think we do." It was time I told my parents I needed space to be myself, to explore art and math and whatever else interested me the way I saw fit.

If I failed, I failed. But I wanted it to be on my own terms. Not because they were pushing me in the direction they felt I should go or telling me what I should deem important.

Mom closed the door behind her and sat down on the bed. She stared at my drawing for almost a full minute, not saying a word. For some reason, I was more unnerved about her seeing it than Grandpa. Maybe because he was an artist, whereas she didn't seem to care about art at all, other than how good it made our house look.

Would she point out spots where I'd messed up? Small flaws I knew peppered the picture?

"It's beautiful," Mom said in a quiet tone.

I paused, blinked.

"Your art has always been so careful," she continued, eyes still locked on the drawing of Matthew. "So . . . precise. It's interesting to see a difference in this piece. The lines aren't as perfectly drawn, but there's more confidence in the picture. I can tell the class has really changed you."

Not just the class. But I couldn't exactly admit to her how I couldn't stop thinking about Matthew, the way he continually pushed me out of my comfort zone. How I now saw everything as being worthy of attention, even if not conventionally beautiful. "I think I'm really good at art," I said to her. "I love it. But Dad makes me feel like it's not important because it's not academic. Why can't I do both?"

Mom sighed and finally looked at me. She rubbed the back of her neck, a sudden weariness in her eyes. "Your father saw how hard it was for me growing up with a parent who was so heavily focused on the arts. Your grandma was the business-minded one in their relationship. She kept the bakery running for many years while your grandpa continued to travel a lot across the country, following his dreams and learning new baking techniques. Leaving me and Grandma alone for weeks at a time."

I didn't know any of this. Mom didn't speak about her childhood often. "So you worry about stability with me? But I'm not a grown-up yet. I just want to enjoy my life right now. Doesn't mean I won't buckle down when I get older."

She gave a small smile. "I know." Then she patted the bed beside her.

I sat down and crossed my legs.

"It took a long time for your grandpa to get his head out of the clouds, Corinne. Well into my adulthood, maybe just a little before you were born. Yeah, he wanted the business and loved it. But he also wanted to still be an artist and live that free lifestyle. It wasn't easy for him to find that balance. He did eventually, though. It just took a long time."

Was she saying that it would be the same for me? I sighed, trying not to feel dejected about her words.

She rubbed my back, the way she used to when I was younger. "Corinne, you're growing up so fast. Sometimes it's easier for your dad and I to still pretend you're a little kid. That we can simply tell you how to live your life and you'll jump right to it. Doesn't help that you were always so eager to please, you did everything we suggested." She laughed. "But now I'm starting to see more of that Walters backbone in you. You're finding your own voice. I might not like it, but I can't exactly argue about it."

A smile crept across my face. "I think it's always been there, Mom. I just didn't know it yet."

Her voice softened. "Honey, I've always loved your art. Always. Even as a little kid, you used to draw me pictures. I've kept them all carefully preserved in an album in my closet."

Now the tears filled my eyes again, and my heart swelled in my chest. "Really?" I squeaked out.

Maybe my mom wasn't as vocal as Matthew's mom about her praise, but she was still proud of me. That sting of jealousy faded completely away, and in its place came a peace I'd been longing for.

"While you got your mother's backbone, you also got your father's competitive streak," she suddenly said with a laugh. "Not sure how that happened, but I know you'll figure out how to balance everything you want. Just give yourself time—life is meant to be savored." Her hand stalled on my lower back, and she glanced back at the picture. "Does he know how you feel?"

I swallowed. "Um, what?"

She raised an eyebrow at me, and I laughed. Yeah, like I could get away with playing dumb. "I wasn't born yesterday," she said, mock affronted. "You're in love with this boy. It shows in all of your careful details. And in that picture you took of him too. I've never seen you like this."

My pulse roared in my ears, and I pressed my suddenly clammy hands to my thighs. Was she right? Had I already jumped off that cliff?

She laughed again and patted my back, standing up. "Don't worry—that will work out too, the way it's supposed to. But do me a favor and don't mention it to your father yet. Poor guy is already struggling with realizing you're growing up. This might push him into heart-attack zone." Her eyes were twinkling, so

I could tell she was joking. "Now, get back to work. You have a project due soon, and all this talking is just getting in the way."

She stroked the back of my head with a soft smile, then left me alone, thoughts swirling like a tornado.

I took a moment to calm myself down and get my emotions under control. Mom's words were a healing balm on my heart. Things weren't perfect, but I knew she supported me. Loved my art and understood my need to keep going with it. And if she would, surely my dad would start to ease up too and stop pushing me so hard on academics. And if not . . . well, all I could do was try.

I moved back to the drawing. A few more touches of shading to the sketch, and it was ready for me to start painting. I grabbed the clean sheet I'd be fusing with Matthew's image of me and started transferring my lines to the paper. At this point, I only had to refer to my picture of him a few times. I'd basically memorized the lines of his face.

I worked late into the night on blocking out the base colors, caught up in the moment, unable to sleep a wink. Unable to tear myself away from rendering Matthew's image as full of life as the original.

I was giving this piece my all. I just prayed it was enough.

"Class, your color studies came out amazing." Teni waved her hand at the pieces hanging around the room. "I want you to take a few minutes and wander around, really examining your fellow students' works. I am so proud of your progress."

The class moved from piece to piece, murmuring discussions to each other as they pointed out various elements in each artwork. I kept a little apart from the group, not wanting my opinion to be influenced by the masses. It really was cool to see how far we'd progressed in such a short time.

And there was only one more week left after this.

A sigh slipped from my lips. It was going to be hard to go back to summer now that our classes were almost over. Maybe I could still keep up the regimen even at home. All I knew was that I couldn't give this up.

"Yours came out great," Matthew said as he inched beside me. "I like the use of red for the sunset-on-a-lake scene."

I shot him a wide smile. "Thanks. I wanted to try something unexpected."

"Ready to work on our project tomorrow?"

I nodded, stomach flaring up in a nervous flutter. "I think so, yes." I'd been spending most of my free time over the last couple of days painting. Tomorrow would be our final meeting, where we would blend the project together and do all the last touches. Then Friday, we'd present it to Teni and hope she liked it.

He smiled, leaning closer. The irises of his eyes seemed a little darker today, like a stormy ocean. I couldn't stop staring at him. "It'll be fine. I'm excited to see your half . . . and to show you mine. I hope you like it."

His breath smelled like fresh mint, and I fought the urge to breathe in deeply. Did he feel the chemistry between us too?

Surely it wasn't just me. My skin was tingling, a sensation that made my stomach flutter even more.

We followed just behind the crowd and kept looking at the other art pieces. Matthew made a few running comments about theme and other elements. I tried to give what I hoped were halfway intelligent answers. But the truth was, I was doing my best not to stand too close to him, afraid he'd be able to read my mind and see all of my jumbled thoughts about him.

Tomorrow was our last day working together, and next week our last class session . . . and then what?

His arm brushed against mine. Was it on purpose? An accident? Argh, my mind was overanalyzing everything now.

Finally we all filtered back to our tables. Teni told us that for our last project, we were open to doing whatever we wanted, using any media we saw fit. But she wanted us to incorporate lessons we'd learned in class so far about color, theme, tone, and media to make our final piece.

I studied my blank paper, just letting my mind wander. I really wanted to make a piece that resonated. But what about?

"Hey," Henry whispered. His eyes twinkled behind his thick glasses. "So, what are you doing your project on? I'm fresh outta ideas."

I laughed. "I was *just* thinking the same thing. I don't have a clue." I turned to Janice. "What about you? Do you have your subject picked out yet?"

She grinned and tucked a strand of red hair that had come out of her ponytail behind her ear. "Nope. I'll just let inspiration come to me as I start drawing out something." Her eyebrow darted up as she looked at me. "So . . . you and Matthew, huh?"

My face instantly flamed. "Um, what?"

Her grin grew wider. "Come on, everyone can see it. The air practically crackles between the two of you. And you've been spending a lot of time together lately."

My first instinct was to flush more and ask if she thought Matthew might feel the same way I did. But then her words kicked in. Everyone could tell how I felt? Really? I frowned. "We're project partners," I said. "Of course we're together."

"Uh-huh." She chuckled. "Hey, nothing bad. I'm just surprised because you guys seem so different."

Henry shoved his glasses up his nose. "That's true. He has that jock vibe going, and you seem very . . ."

"Nerdy?" I filled in lightly, though my heart wasn't feeling that way. It was easy to get caught up in my own bubble and think we had potential, think we had chemistry. But when push came to shove, even almost complete strangers noticed how different we are. And I wasn't just talking about skin color.

"Opposites do attract," Janice declared.

I wasn't ready to hear their thoughts on why we wouldn't work. I already had my own concerns about it and had been torn over the last few days between focusing on those issues and ignoring them.

Regardless, I was going to talk to Matthew first before I

dished my feelings to anyone, especially fellow art students. I needed to see how he felt . . . and then we could take it from there. No sense starting the rumor mill buzzing—I knew how fast gossip could spread around here.

"Matthew and I are just friends," I said in a firm tone. Maybe that would stop them from talking about us. "The only thing we have going on right now is our art project."

Janice's face froze for a second, and she and Henry paused. I saw Matthew walk by, his back stiff as a board, shoulders tight. He moved to the back of the room and flipped through some magazines. His posture appeared casual; I couldn't tell what he was thinking or feeling.

Had he overheard me? My heart sank.

Then another guy in class came over and started talking to him. They both laughed. No tension in Matthew's eyes whatsoever.

If he had overheard, he didn't seem upset by what I'd said. Maybe I'd been imagining his pain at my words . . . maybe even imagining he cared about me like that at all.

Ugh, I was driving myself crazy!

I turned back to my project, staring at my blank canvas for what felt like forever. I drew a line, then erased it. Drew another. Erased that too. Nothing was flowing.

I couldn't stop thinking about him.

Finally, thankfully, class ended. I gathered my stuff up as fast as I could. Perhaps I could talk to Matthew and see how he felt about everything. Ask what he'd overheard. Maybe I could explain my words somehow without giving away my ever-growing feelings for him.

But when I finished packing up and looked toward his station, he was already gone.

Chapter ● Seventeen

I could barely hear anything because my pulse was roaring so loudly in my ears. My hands shook so hard I was afraid the painting would fly right out of them and into the thick green grass.

Relax, I told myself. It would be fine.

But I couldn't help but be nervous as I walked into Teni's studio the next afternoon. The air-conditioning was a refreshing blast in my face and across my bare arms and legs, but it didn't ease my nervousness.

I was nervous to see Matthew's painting.

I was nervous about him seeing mine.

But mostly, I was nervous about just seeing *him*. He hadn't texted me yesterday or today. Maybe he really was mad at me.

Or maybe I'd blown everything out of proportion and read

into something that wasn't there—the guy could have been busy, for all I knew. He did have two sisters to watch. I knew how hard it could be to juggle everything.

I grabbed a chair and sat, waiting for him. I was a few minutes early, hoping to give myself a chance to chill out before he arrived. No way did I want to seem so nervous.

I pressed my hands to my thighs and drew slow, deep breaths. In, out. In, out. It was all going to be fine. I simply had to relax.

The door opened, and my heart stuttered. I looked over to see Matthew stroll in, his painting covered by a large piece of paper. He gave me a small smile and headed toward me.

My lungs squeezed to the size of grapes, and I could hardly draw in a breath. His eyes locked me in and wouldn't let me go.

This was just crazy! I blinked and dragged my gaze away from his. "You all ready?" I asked.

We took our respective pieces, still covered, over to a large expanse of table, where we would do our splicing together and the final touches. We both paused, looking at each other. A light blush rode high on his tanned cheekbones, and my fingers itched to touch his skin.

I fisted them at my sides.

"You go first," I said.

"No, you," he countered with an eyebrow raised in challenge.

We both laughed. The tension seemed to crack apart, and our shoulders relaxed at the same time.

"Okay, we'll reveal them together," I offered. "One . . . two . . . three."

We uncovered our images and fixed our attention on each other's paintings.

My breath locked in my lungs. I couldn't stop staring. Matthew had used bold, abstract lines to capture my face—his typical postmodern style, with a bit of flair. But somehow, you could still easily see it was me. There was a little more realism in my eyes, in the crook of my mouth, which turned up in the corners.

My half-portrait held a hint of mischievousness. Even without being classically rendered, without all the careful lines and perspective, it was strongly apparent it was me. He'd nailed it.

My hand fluttered to my chest, and I kept staring at it. Wow. No wonder Teni had insisted he be in the competition. The piece was *good*. Sophisticated. Edgy yet appealing, accessible.

"It's amazing," I finally said. "I can't believe . . . I just don't know what to say."

Then I realized he hadn't looked up at me yet. He was still staring hard at my image, a slight frown on his face. My stomach pinched. Was he unhappy with the way I'd painted him? I'd tried to let myself fall into the painting, to feel it and not worry so hard about rigid, perfect linework. I'd poured all of my emotion into his eyes, wanting those to ring true. But maybe I'd failed.

He finally turned his eyes to me, fixing me in that rich blue stare. "No one's ever . . ." He paused. "No one has ever done a piece like this of me before."

Suddenly shy, I found myself asking, "Do you like it?"

"I love it," he said simply.

I fought to keep a stupid grin off my face as we looked back down at our paintings. My heart was racing, but this time out of excitement. "I think we have a real chance of winning."

"I do too. Let's splice these together and finish this up."

We spent the next half hour carefully trimming our images, pasting them onto a fresh piece of paper so our faces melded into each other, each of us one half of a larger face. It was amazing once I saw how they worked together, how the lines of our jaws, our brows touched. All our careful planning beforehand had worked out.

The center seams of our lips kissed each other right in the middle of the painting. My skin grew hot and a little itchy as I stared, transfixed, at our mouths.

What would it be like to really kiss Matthew? Would his mouth taste as minty as it smells? How would it feel to have his hands on my upper arms, sliding to my back? To tangle my fingers in his thick hair and have our mouths draw closer—

"Corinne," he whispered right beside me.

I jumped, blinked, heart racing. I knew guilt was written all over my face. My thoughts had been wandering down to a place I shouldn't be going. Not with my art partner. *Pull yourself together!* "Um, sorry. I got distracted. What's up?"

He gave me a weird look. "Are you ready to finish the background?"

We'd decided we would do the background of the painting together, using random colors to highlight and stretch across both halves of the image's background. The unifying piece that would tie everything in together.

I gave a mechanical nod and grabbed the paints. My hands only trembled a little bit as I squirted paint onto our palettes.

We worked in silence for another twenty minutes or so on the background. Our paint lines blended and blurred over each other. He went right over a fresh red line I'd done with a dark blue, so I crossed over it with red again.

He laughed. "So it's gonna be like that, huh?"

That started it. Our laughter built louder as we dabbed and painted and plopped colors onto the page. It was goofy. Fun. I'd never done art like this before. But somehow, it worked. It was a chaotic, bright background that interconnected our styles.

"That color looks awful," I said, nodding my head at the top right color. All our layering in that spot had made a dumpy shade of brown.

"Huh. Well, I blame you," he retorted with a straight face.

Before I realized what I was doing, I raised my brush and put a glop of purple paint on his cheek.

His eyes slitted in playful menace. He lifted his brush and took a step toward me.

I squealed and jumped back. "Sorry, sorry!" I said with a laugh. I grabbed a paper towel and wet it, then came toward him with a hands-in-the-air symbol of truce. My hands shook a little as I wiped the paint off his cheek.

Matthew froze and quickly inhaled. I darted my eyes to his. His pupils were large, filled with an intensity I'd never seen before. It shocked the air out of my lungs.

"Corinne," he whispered. His voice was gravelly.

A bubble of excitement swelled in my chest. There was something there, crackling between us. No way was it just in my head. I could see that now with full certainty.

"What?" I whispered back.

"When this project is over . . ." He paused, licked his lower lip in a nervous tic. The action drew my eyes to his mouth again.

You guys seem so different. Janice's words echoed in my head. The words washed over me like a cold shower. Too different to make it work long-term, if that was even what he wanted? What if my feelings were stronger than his?

Or worse, what if we both felt the same way but couldn't seem to mesh our real lives together once school started? I wasn't certain how two people so different could make a relationship work.

Would we just fall apart, disintegrate into nothingness?

Suddenly I wasn't sure I was ready to hear whatever he had to say. Shame filled me about my intense fear, but I didn't want to ruin this perfect moment by taking it down a path when we weren't quite ready to accept its consequences. After all, Matthew might think he liked me now, but maybe that was just because of the intensity of our project, the forced togetherness. Working one on one for an extended period of time could create an intimacy that might not last once reality crashed back in.

How would he feel when it was all over? Would he still want to hang out with me? Despite everything right now, in this moment, I still had a hard time consistently reading him. He didn't seem to have the consistent intense emotions about me that I did about him.

All these questions were making me frustrated, dizzy. I needed time to think.

"Um, we need to finish the background," I said, giving a forced smile. "Our project is almost done. I really think Teni will like it."

"But we need to talk first," he said, not bothering with a smile. His eyes were locked on mine. "I want to know—"

A song vibrated from my pocket. My phone.

The moment was broken. Matthew stepped back, frustration clear on his face, and I tugged my cell out. It was my mom.

"Hey, Corinne," Mom said. "Sorry to interrupt you, but Charlie's acting up at home, and your father needs you to help watch him while he finishes work. Your brother is refusing to leave the house unless you take him somewhere."

"Okay," I told her, then hung up. I was simultaneously relieved and irritated. Charlie always did have the worst timing. And yet this would give me a little bit of a reprieve to think about everything. "I'm sorry. I have to go in a minute. Gotta watch my brother." I glanced at the painting. "I think we're about done here."

"Yeah, I guess so." Matthew's words had a slight strain around the edges. He turned his back to me and started cleaning up the brushes and palettes.

Great. I'd ticked him off.

"Matthew—" I started.

He waved a hand without looking at me. "You should hurry so you can get home. I'll take care of cleaning everything up." Yup, there was definitely an edge of frostiness in his voice.

My heart thudded dully. "Okay. Thanks."

He shrugged, still keeping his back to me.

I gathered my things and headed to the door. When I got there, I paused and turned. I watched him for a moment, drinking in the way he moved. How he absorbed himself fully in whatever he was doing, whether it was art or basketball or something as simple as cleaning.

"I'll see you tomorrow," I whispered, then left.

The walk home felt like it took forever. My brain wouldn't stop throwing questions at me. My heart wouldn't stop screaming that I was a coward. I wanted to just curl up in my bed and sleep it all away.

Charlie almost attacked me when I got home, tugging me inside. "I'm so bored and Maxine isn't home and Dad won't let me go anywhere by myself. Can we go to the park? Please?" He sounded so pathetic and needy that I couldn't help but agree.

The rest of my afternoon I spent watching Charlie play with his sun-powered car.

Unable to forget the disappointment in Matthew's eyes.

Chapter ● Eighteen

love that subject," Janice said to me, pointing at the painting I was fleshing out with undertones. "What gave you the idea?"

I tilted my head and stared at the image. Inspiration had finally hit me at the beginning of class, and I'd furiously sketched the graffiti wall I'd seen on my walk that one evening. Something about it had resonated with me, stuck with me. I knew this had to be my last class project.

I explained how I'd gone walking and had taken pictures of stuff I saw around Lakewood.

"What a great idea," she said, giving a nod of appreciation. Today Janice had on a flowing blue dress and her red hair was twisted into braids. She looked the image of a typical artist—or at least, what would have been my image before this class.

Teni's workshop—Matthew's art—had changed me.

Now I saw art in everything, the beautiful and the mundane. The ugly and scary and strange. It was exciting, the realization that inspiration lay all around me.

"You should give it a try sometime," I said. "I think you'd enjoy it. Challenges your artistic eye."

"Would you come out with me? I'd love to see you in composition mode and study your ideas a little more."

I blinked. "Really?" Janice was looking to me as an expert? Warmth flooded my chest. "I'd be happy to."

She nodded, and I turned my attention back to my painting, pleasure flushing my cheeks.

For the hundredth time today, my gaze darted to Matthew's back. He was fully focused on his image, an unusually realistic rendering of his twin sisters at the park near his house, smiling at each other in what was probably a rare moment of serenity for them. For his media he was using pencil only, and right now he was crosshatching shades in their hair.

He hadn't looked at me once.

I pushed aside my anxiety about it and tried to focus on my painting. We were presenting our final project to Teni after class today. And when that was done, I was going to make him talk to me. No way could I leave everything like this—tense, awkward. I still had no idea what to say, but at least I could listen to him.

I'd cut him off so rudely yesterday. No wonder he was frustrated with me.

The rest of class went surprisingly fast. It was a bittersweet feeling when Teni announced it was done. Monday would be our last session, and we could wrap up our in-class projects then.

"I'm so excited to see how you have grown," Teni said. She walked up and down the aisles, taking in the drawings and paintings and such that were on easels scattered across the room. "You have all pushed yourselves and expanded not only your technical skills, but your artistic sensibilities. I am honored to have had you in my class."

I heard a small sniffle from behind me. Apparently Janice was feeling as unhappy about it as I was. My chest had this bubble of sadness in it. Funny how art had become important so quickly. A few weeks in the program didn't feel like enough.

I stared at my painting in progress. I'd accomplished a lot today, and it would be pretty close to done on Monday. I was really going to miss losing myself in art. Yes, I still loved math and academics, but it wasn't the same. Those successes were expected. The rush I got from my art turning out the way I'd envisioned was nothing like I'd ever experienced before.

With a reluctant sigh, I cleaned my brushes and palette and straightened up my station. All too soon I'd be back to reality, where academics would be my biggest focus. How did Matthew handle it? Like me, he strove hard in his area of interest. Yet it was obvious he still made time for art—he went to galleries, took photographs, drew and painted when he could.

Maybe I could too. If I approached it just right, showed that I wouldn't be giving up my academic pursuits, that I could balance it all, plus still keep up art, my parents wouldn't be on my case for not devoting all my time to the French club or to the mathlete team. The bubble of sorrow shrank in my chest and was replaced by a tinge of hope.

Teni waved at me and Matthew, and my heart gave an irregular thud of panic as I shuffled my way to the front of the room. Would she like this project better than the first one we'd discussed with her? By tacit agreement, Matthew and I hadn't shown her our work yet, wanting to surprise her and get her honest, initial reaction.

Her face lit up as we neared. Matthew stood a few inches from me, and I could feel the heat pouring off his body. I fought the urge to sway closer to him. I missed the feel of his hands in mine. Crazy how I'd come to crave his nearness.

"So," Teni said with an excited clap of her hands. "Let me see the project. I've been dying of anticipation, especially since you two haven't shown me a thing." She gave us a mock frown. "I had hoped to be more of a guiding light in the project, but it seems you were both able to make it work okay without my help?"

I bit my lip. Matthew grabbed the covered easel nearest us and took off the top layer of cardboard.

Teni blinked, then stared for a good long minute. I worried my fingers, keeping my hands tightened in front of me. Matthew stood completely still, but I could see a small clenching of his jaw.

He was nervous too. That thought, strangely enough, helped ease some of my apprehension. We were in this together.

I reached over and brushed his arm with the tips of my fingers. He looked down at me, the frown line between his brows easing up. Then he gave me a genuine smile—small, but real.

My heart thudded in relief. I swallowed and dropped my arm to my side. Oh, I'd missed that smile. Had needed it more than I'd realized. I gave him a tiny, secret grin in return.

"This is wonderful," Teni finally said. She turned her attention to us, and a smile slid across her face. She waved a bejeweled hand at the painting. "After seeing this, I'm definitely glad you two decided to change your subject matter. This final product is daring, intimate. I can see pieces of both of you in here, yet there are also spots that blend you two together. Seeing how you envision each other, how your faces came together to create one cohesive image. I love the wild background, as well. Risky, but it has a great chance in the competition." She reached over and clasped one of my hands, then one of his. "I am honored to present this to the committee. I can tell how hard you both worked on this . . . and you did it together. I think this is exactly what they're looking for."

She didn't know how hard we'd struggled to get to this point, but in this moment, that didn't matter. All the stress and strain and time had been worth it. The project was ready, and I was proud of it.

"Now, go. Celebrate your success." Her eyes twinkled, and

she dropped our hands. "I'll take care of this. Hopefully I'll have good news for you soon."

Matthew and I gathered our things. My head was so light I was afraid I'd float right out of the building. Fear would settle in later, I knew. But right now, I was riding the wave of happiness, for once completely satisfied with my art.

Not critiquing its flaws or trying to push ever closer to perfection.

No. Just enjoying it in its messy, fun imperfection. We'd had fun yesterday putting it together. Until I'd cut him off and things had gotten weird.

When we stepped outside into the overcast sky, I said, "Matthew, wait. Are you . . . busy right now?" My face burned, and I steeled myself for possible rejection. After all, it was my fault things were the way they were between us.

He stopped in place and turned to face me. I couldn't read the emotion in his eyes, but I could tell he was feeling a lot of things right now. His lips thinned. "Do you want to talk?"

I knew what he was saying. He wanted to finish the conversation we'd started yesterday . . . the one I both craved and feared.

I nodded. I owed him that much, at least—to not chicken out.

Gradually the tension around his mouth and eyes relaxed. "Ice cream?"

The tension faded from my limbs. "Sounds great."

There was an ice-cream shop a couple of blocks from the studio. Matthew and I walked side by side, bags slung over our backs. I sent my parents a quick text letting them know where I was going.

The line wasn't too bad when we arrived. Matthew ordered ice cream for both of us—he refused to let me pay, which made me feel guilty but also flattered—and we settled in at an outdoor table under a large umbrella. Hopefully the rain would hold off; the clouds were heavy, but nothing had come yet.

We ate in silence for a few minutes, enjoying our ice cream.

"I can't believe the project is all done," he said after he polished off the last of his chocolate and vanilla swirl cone. "And class is almost over too."

"And school starts back up again in just over a month. The summer's flying by way too quickly." I sighed and scooped out my last bite of banana, dipping it into the rich hot fudge that slid along the side of the plastic container. It was exquisite. I closed my eyes and savored the bite.

A small sound made me open my eyes. I looked over at Matthew. He had a deep frown line between his brows.

"What's wrong?" I asked him.

"I need to ask you something." His tone was as serious as I'd ever heard it, and I knew the conversation was going to head into *that* zone.

My heart stalled, then restarted again, giving a furious thump below my rib cage. "Okay." With slightly shaky hands, I pushed my empty ice-cream container away from me.

"How do you feel about me?"

His blunt words actually made my cheeks burn. Oh, great—he was putting it on my shoulders to go first? My initial instinct was to throw it back on him, to make him answer. But for some reason, I felt like I needed to be honest. Even if it was me putting myself out there.

Matthew deserved it. He'd been honest with me from the start.

I swallowed, pressed my hands together in my lap. "Um. At first I thought you were just a jock—only into sports and not caring much about anything else." I forced myself to keep speaking, eyes fixed on the table since I was too afraid to look up into his eyes. "But now I know there's more to you. A lot more than I ever would have guessed." I gave a guilty laugh. "Guess that's what I get for making assumptions."

"Corinne," he said, sliding across the bench until our thighs were almost touching. My leg began to tremble. I glanced up. His eyes were piercing, and it was like a wall had crumbled between us. I could read every emotion on his face.

The power, the intensity of it took my breath away.

He grabbed my fingers, rested them between his warm palms. His thumb stroked the top of my hand. My breath came in short, nervous pants. "I don't want us to stop seeing each other when class is done."

A shaky laugh slipped out of my mouth. "Then let's hope we win." A flippant answer, but I couldn't help it. I was so nervous.

He leaned closer until his face was inches from mine. He

shook his head and gave a crooked grin, rolling his eyes. "You know what I mean."

"I know." A thousand thoughts battered against my mind all at once. I wanted him to lean closer and feel those full lips press against mine. Wanted to give in to the need filling my heart. And yet . . . all those doubts that had plagued me endlessly were still there, and I couldn't push them away. If I was this nervous, this uncertain about us being together, wasn't that a bad sign?

"I want to see you outside of art class. Outside of school. I want us to go on a real date together." He stared into my eyes. "I'd like to meet your family and friends. I've had a lot of fun hanging out with you because of this project. I don't want that to stop."

I bit my lower lip. "I have too. But . . . we're so different."

His fingers stilled. "Not as different as you think," he responded. "Our art project proves we can make it work if we both want to."

"And look at how hard that was," I said. "It took us so long to even compromise on it." My heart raced, and I knew he could feel the shaking in my hand. Sadness filled my chest, and my heart sank. Reality swept over me in a bitter wash of color. "We could see each other this summer, and everything would be just like it is now. But what happens when school starts and real life picks back up again? For example, whose lunch table do we sit at—your friends or mine?"

His jaw tightened. "Does it matter? We can alternate. Or sit at our own."

"Your friends hate school. Mine hate sports," I continued. "So who would we hang out with on weekends? And when I have my academic challenges, you won't be there—because you'll be busy with basketball. And I can't cheer on your baskets because my parents expect me to spend my free time on math."

Rain began to patter against the umbrella. I glanced around and realized everyone else had vacated the outdoor patio. It was just us, in the rain, a sheet of water blanketing us from the rest of the world.

"Why do you focus so much on how different we are?" he challenged. I could see a spark of fire in his eyes. His hand tightened around mine. "What does any of that matter in the end? If we like each other, it will all work out. Yeah, it's a risk, but isn't everything that's good in life?"

I bit back a sigh. It was easy for him to talk about taking risks. He'd practically been born a risk taker. My nature was to be cautious and thorough. To plan and know exactly what I was getting into.

"I'm not just making this up in my head—I can tell I'm not the only one here," he said in a softer voice. One hand reached up and cupped my cheek.

A big part of me wanted to let all of my fears go and lean into his embrace. But one of us had to be realistic here. I'd seen friends dive headfirst off the cliff and come out bruised and battered because they weren't sensible. Like Ava, for instance—her last relationship had ended in a nasty fight because they'd both wanted different things. She'd cried for weeks afterward.

If that happened to me and Matthew, it would crush me.

"You're not making it up," I said. "I feel it too. But liking each other isn't enough to make us work."

He thinned his lips and dropped his hand from my cheek, which cooled instantly. Then he stood and dumped his napkin in a nearby garbage can. Rain pounded on his head, slicking his hair to the sides of his face. Hot tears burned the insides of my eyes.

I wasn't a coward this time, hadn't run away from the conversation. I'd been honest and faced the truth he didn't want to face. But it didn't make my words hurt any less. It was one thing to let everything go and take a risk in art. Another thing completely to take a risk in a relationship.

"I hear what you're saying. You've made your point. I gotta go." His words were quiet and flat. The warmth in his eyes was gone.

My chest tightened in remorse.

Then he left, and I stared at him walking off in the rain. I wanted to call for him to come back, but I kept my mouth shut. It was better this way—I'd saved us a lot of pain in the long term.

It wasn't until I felt wetness plop onto my shirt that I realized I was crying.

Chapter ● Nineteen

A soft knock on my bedroom door jarred me out of my sleepy stupor. I glanced at the clock—it was close to midnight. Who was up this late?

The door peeked open. "Corinne, are you awake?"

"Charlie?" I rubbed a hand over my eyes.

The door closed behind him. I flipped on my bedside lamp, bathing the room in a soft golden glow.

Charlie's face was drawn. He shuffled over to the chair at my desk. "Did I wake you up?"

"I was just kinda lying here dozing." I'd gone to bed at ten but had lain here for well over an hour, unable to sleep, still haunted by Matthew's eyes earlier today right before he'd walked away. Tomorrow was Saturday. I had to work at the bakery in the morning. But I couldn't get my brain to shut off. "What's wrong?"

Charlie had never come to my room this late. Had to be a big deal, whatever the problem was. Concern for my little brother filled my chest.

He sighed. "I need to talk to you. I couldn't fall asleep."

I swung my legs over the side of the bed. "What's going on?"

He crossed his arms over his chest. There was so much misery on his face that my heart went out to him. "It's about Maxine. I don't know what to do. She . . ." He paused. "Well, I saw her earlier today hanging out with some other guys at our school. And then one of them left but the other stayed, and they were sitting really close, and then the guy tried to hold her hand."

Poor guy. "How did it make you feel?"

"Jealous!" he said, then dropped his voice, gaze darting to the door. Neither one of us wanted to wake our parents. "I realized I was really jealous. I didn't want him holding her hand."

"So why don't you do something about it?" I grabbed my pillow and tucked it on my lap.

"Like what? I can't tell her she can't have other guy friends."

I tilted my head. "What is it you want from your relationship with her?"

He shrugged. "I dunno."

"I think you do know." I raised an eyebrow. "You need to face it, Charlie. Face how you feel. Maxine has liked you for a while now."

"No, she hasn't," he protested. "We're just friends."

"You are friends. But she wanted more. And when she realized you didn't want more with her . . ." I let my words trail off. He knew what I was saying.

"But . . . maybe I do want more," he said. "Maybe I just didn't realize it until now. Until I saw another guy with her."

"Have you told her how you feel?"

His face scrunched up. "Uh, no. I can't."

"Why?"

"Because it'll ruin everything. And . . . I don't know what I'll do if she's not my friend anymore." His voice was so low I had to strain to hear him. "And what if she doesn't even like me anymore, and I tell her, and we stop being friends?"

My heart broke for him. "Oh, Charlie—girls don't get over crushes that quickly. Trust me."

"They don't?" His face became a little less mopey.

I shook my head. "If she likes you, that won't go away for a while. But it will if you don't do something about it. You gotta tell her soon. Otherwise, you're going to be sitting here with this horrible feeling, regretting not sharing your feelings. And then it really *will* ruin your friendship."

Suddenly I thought of Matthew. Had he been this nervous to talk to me today? I blinked. My eyes began to sting.

Stop it, I ordered myself. This was about Charlie, not about me.

Charlie gave a short nod. "What do I say?"

"Keep it simple. Tell her you realized you like her and you want to date her." My stomach gave a horrible twist. Basically the same convo I'd had earlier today. And it had gone so badly.

Because I was too practical to just jump in and trust.

But our situations were not the same, I reminded myself. My brother and Maxine had been friends forever. Had tons in common. They had a solid foundation, whereas Matthew and I didn't. A relationship between me and Matthew would be a huge risk. Charlie's relationship wouldn't be.

He scrubbed a hand over the back of his neck. In that moment, he looked less like a little lost kid and more like a guy who was growing into a teenager. My little brother, almost as tall as me. Soon he'd be navigating this on his own.

"It'll go fine," I told him, hoping to ease the worry in his eyes. "She still likes you. She just needs to hear you say it."

He stood and then, to my surprise, gave me a quick hug. Now I really was shocked—Charlie wasn't a hugger at all. "Thanks," he said. "I'll tell her tomorrow."

He quietly closed the door behind him.

I lay back in bed, staring at the ceiling. I wish my situation were that easy—that I could just say, "Hey, Matthew. Who cares if it's a risk? Let's give it a shot."

But there were so many factors that went against us. And that didn't even touch how my dad would react if I started dating a guy. He'd never let me get alone time with Matthew, insisting my schoolwork should always come first.

What did any of my struggle matter anyway? After that blowout today, it seemed pretty final. Matthew wasn't going to ask me to hang out anymore. No more impromptu texts or visits to the art gallery. Our art classes were ending on Monday, and if he and I didn't win the competition, I wouldn't see him again until school started. We'd go back to the way we were before.

No, not back to that. It would be even worse, because back then, I didn't know what I was missing. His smile, his view of the world. The fluttery way he made me feel.

My chest grew heavy with sorrow. In this moment, when I could be completely honest with myself, I couldn't fathom going back to school and seeing him in class, in the lunchroom, remembering how things were this summer and knowing our distance was my fault. This would hurt far, far worse than I'd even realized.

So much for my noble ideals.

I grabbed a pillow and slammed it over my face, squealing with frustration. Why did everything turn so messy when you got older? And would my mind ever stop thinking about him?

Probably not for a long, long time.

"I missed you so much!" I said, hugging Ava as tight as I could.

She wrapped her arms around me and laughed, but the sound came out like a wheeze. "Corinne, I can't breathe."

I loosened up a fraction. "Oh, sorry." Pulling back, I held her at arm's length. She looked the same, but there was a sparkle in her eye, an easiness to her stance that hadn't been there before. Scotland had been good for her.

She did a few model poses for me, showing off her new kilt with a giggle. "Do you like it? It's done in our family's tartan pattern!"

I led her over to my bed. "You have to tell me all about it. We have some time before Mom gets us for dinner." It was a Thursday, but Mom was getting off work early, so we were doing our family dinner tonight. A total bonus that Ava was crashing at our house this evening too.

I'd been anticipating this happy visit for what felt like forever. Between waiting anxiously for news about the competition and getting dead silence from Matthew since art class had ended last week, I'd been in a total moody slump.

We spent the next half hour talking about Ava's vacation—how her parents had found the origins of her family tree, including the small hometown her ancestors had lived in since the Middle Ages.

"Wow," I breathed. "How amazing is that? What was it like, standing in the street of that hometown, knowing your family had lived there for generations?"

She shook her head, awe pouring from her eyes. "It was . . . unreal. The place felt ancient. I don't know how to describe it. Yeah, there were some modern conveniences, but so many of the buildings were hundreds of years old. I want to go back."

"I would too. Did you meet any other cute guys while you were there? Whatever happened to the British guy in your hotel?"

She laughed. "Oh! I forgot all about him. He left for home the day after. But it didn't matter, because there was this one guy . . ." Ava told me all about the local who showed her around. "He had the most amazing blue eyes I'd ever seen."

Matthew's eyes popped into my mind.

"What's wrong?" Ava frowned. "You got this . . . sad look on your face."

I hadn't wanted to bother her with the details of what had happened. So I'd kept it all to myself. I tried to sum it up in as few words as possible, downplaying the way my heart couldn't seem to let him go. "Anyway, it was for the best," I said, waving my hand in a dismissive manner. "We never would have made it work once school started."

"You didn't even try?" She crossed her arms, disappointment clear on her face. "You just gave up?"

Defensiveness crept in. "I didn't *give up*. There wasn't anything *to* give up. We were just partners, and now that's done." But even as I said it, my heart squeezed in regret. I couldn't deny it—I missed talking to him. Missed hearing his loud laugh.

She shook her head. "Girl, I don't understand you."

"Look at how well it worked out for you," I pointed out, reminding her of her ex. "You were heartbroken for weeks. I held you as you cried." My own tears started rushing to the surface. I blinked them back.

"Oh, Corinne, you're not using that as a reason not to see him, are you? David and I never had a chance to begin with—we were doomed to fail before we even started. And not because we were so different," she pressed on, holding up a hand to stop me from speaking, "but because he never liked me as much as I liked him."

I stayed silent. Ava had never told me that before. "But . . . you said that . . ."

She swallowed, and a flush crept across her cheeks. "I said that because I was mortified. I was practically in love with him. It was easier at the time to blame our differences. I realize now that if he'd cared about me as much as I had about him, we would have made it work."

I pressed a shaky hand to my throat. Regret slammed me in the chest, almost winded me. What had I done? Was it a mistake to toss away our chance at a relationship because of my fear?

Ava's face fell, and she studied me. "Oh, honey." She rubbed my arm. "You fell hard, didn't you."

There was a knock on the door.

I blinked and swiped at my face, forcing a smile to my lips. "Come in."

My mom came in, the phone cradled to her chest. She had a strange look on her face. "It's for you."

Who was calling me on the home phone? All of my friends had my cell phone number. I took it from her, shooting a quick glance at her hovering in the doorway, then at Ava. "Hello? This is Corinne."

"Corinne, this is Teni."

Instantly my lungs froze, air locked tight inside. My hand shook.

The contest.

I dragged in a ragged breath, brain scrabbling for words.

"Um, yes. Hello. It's me." Lame! She already knew that. *Get it together!*

"I have some news. Your art piece with Matthew . . . has won first prize!" Her voice grew more excited as she talked, but I stopped understanding her, my brain catching and repeating her words.

We won.

We won!

"Omigod!" I said in a huge rush, squeezing Ava with my free hand. "Omigod! I can't believe it! Wait, can you say all of that again? I think I blacked out for a second."

Teni laughed and repeated herself. She told me when and where the gallery exhibit would be and gave me all the details. In the fall, our piece would be in a national art magazine with over a million subscribers—that part made me nearly faint. Then she asked to talk to my mom again so she could set up the flight and hotel for us.

I gave her back the phone. Then I cupped my hands over my mouth and squealed as loud as I could.

"Corinne!" Ava said, eyes huge. "Is it . . ."

I nodded. Hot tears of joy sprung to my eyes and I let them course down my face. My hands trembled from sheer elation. I couldn't believe it. Our piece had won.

Mom cupped her hand over the receiver. Her eyes shone with pride. "Congrats, honey! I'll come back in in a little bit to tell you about the hotel and flight details." She closed the door behind her.

Ava captured me in a huge hug. "I knew it! You're amazing, and I knew you'd win!"

I drew in a few slow breaths. "I wasn't sure. I knew there would be some amazing pieces out there." Wow. I grabbed my phone and instinctively started to enter in Matthew's number. Then I froze.

We'd won. But did that mean he'd want to talk to me? I could still see the hurt and frustration in his eyes after our argument. He hadn't even looked my way on Monday except to give me a polite nod.

I put my phone down and looked at Ava. Suddenly I felt lost. The other person I most wanted to share this moment with was . . . him. And I'd pushed him away.

"You should call him," she said in a low whisper. Sympathy poured from her eyes. "I'm sure he'll want to hear from you. He might be doing the same thing you are, not sure if he should call or text."

"I don't know . . ." Yes, we won, but did that change anything between us? I had to admit it to myself, to stop denying how I really felt—I was flat-out scared. Ava had clarified why she and her ex hadn't worked. But that didn't mean Matthew and I would.

Then again, I hadn't even given it a fair chance. It had failed because I'd failed it—I'd failed us.

"Win him back," Ava suddenly declared. Her eyes grew heated and her words passionate. "He loves you. You love him."

"Wait, no one said love—"

"Puh-lease. It is written all over your face." She snorted and stood, staring down at me, still perched on the edge of the bed. "Show him you care. Let him know how important he is to you! Call him." She paused. "Or even better, show him in New York at the exhibit. Then he has to listen to you." Her face softened as she stared over my shoulder, eyes dreamy. "And then you can tell him how you feel, and he will take you in his arms and kiss you."

I wanted to laugh at her for being such a romantic. But I couldn't. I knew that was what I wanted—for him to still care about me. For me to let go of my fears, step to the edge of that cliff, and jump.

A small bead of hope started in my chest. I looked at Ava. "Maybe I will."

And if I did, would Matthew still be there?

Or had he already started moving on?

Chapter ● Twenty

Three weeks later

"Holy cow," Charlie breathed. "New York City is crazy."

I was about to reply, but a line of cabs swerved by the corner where we stood, honking like crazy. Midafternoon light filled the street and sidewalk, casting glows on everything, making signs shinier and even more eye-catching. Business people bustled all around us, their feet flying by in high heels or dressy shoes.

It was amazing.

"Stay together," Dad warned. He had Mom's hand practically locked in his, like he was afraid of losing her. His eyes hadn't strayed far from me and my brother.

I laughed. "No one's going to snatch us off the street," I said to him.

We crossed the street and kept walking. My pale blue dress floated around my legs, wisps of fabric teasing my skin as they flipped and whipped on the breeze. My shoes were cute flat sandals—I'd gone for practical instead of trendy, since I knew we'd be walking here today.

One more block and we'd be there.

We'd arrived in the city last night, tired but excited. Dad wouldn't let me and Charlie wander around alone, so we'd spent the evening in the hotel room, talking about the exhibit. Wondering what it would be like.

I hadn't talked to anyone about the question nearest and dearest to my heart right now—if Matthew would actually be there. And if he'd listen to me.

This morning had included a little sightseeing, then back to the room to get ready. And now we were about to enter the gallery. Where our winning piece would be hanging on a wall for everyone to see.

My stomach pitched. I pressed shaking hands to my belly, stopping right before we went inside the trendy brick building. Oh wow, I hadn't anticipated this nervousness.

Mom rested a hand on my shoulders, her eyes filled with warmth. "It'll be fine," she whispered. "People are going to love it."

I nodded, sucking in a few breaths.

Dad paused, staring down at me. "Hey. I know I don't say this a lot but . . . I'm really proud of you, Corinne. You worked hard and you deserve this. I can't wait to see it." Sincerity shone in his eyes.

Getting that praise from my dad eased some of the uneasy tension in me. My heart swelled, and I gave him a quick nod—I wasn't sure I could muster any words out of my tight throat right now.

He squeezed my arm and smiled, stepping back. Then we all headed inside, out of the heat of the summer sun.

Cool air whirled around us instantly, and I blinked to acclimate my eyes to the dimmer lighting in here. There was a narrow staircase on the left with a sign indicating the gallery was upstairs, so up we climbed until we reached the gallery's glass doors. We entered. The building's walls were rough brick, a long, wide room stretching all the way to the back. Paintings were scattered everywhere, all shapes and sizes. Chandeliers dangled from the ceiling, and small chairs and couches were scattered throughout.

It was amazing.

"Welcome," a short round woman said, popping up out of nowhere beside us. She had on a pair of black pants with a ruffled white shirt, and her hair was pulled up in a messy but cute bun. "Can I help you?"

"We're here because of the high school art competition," Mom said proudly. She inclined her head toward me. "Corinne Walters, one of the winners this year."

The woman clapped. "Wonderful! We've been waiting for you. Please, come this way. We have a table of refreshments all set up."

Charlie tugged at his necktie as he slumped beside me. "Think I can take this off yet?" he asked.

"Maybe soon," I whispered back. My phone vibrated. I took it out and smiled, then handed it to Charlie. "Guess who."

He swallowed and reached for the phone. "It's her," he breathed. His fingers flew across the buttons as he texted Maxine back.

I couldn't help but feel proud of him. After our talk, he'd approached Maxine and flat-out told her that he realized he liked her and he didn't want her dating anyone else. According to what I could pry out of him, she'd apparently rolled her eyes, told him it was about time, then planted a huge kiss on him.

While I was happy for them, I couldn't help but think of my own situation. Wondering if I was going to get my first kiss anytime soon. Or if Matthew would even listen to me. I scanned the room, looking for him. He wasn't here.

Disappointment filled my chest. I made my way to the refreshments table and grabbed a cup of punch. There were several adults standing there, and they all came up and talked rapidly to me, thanking me for showing up, for entering the competition, gushing about how much they loved the project.

I tried to shove aside my own personal turmoil and focus on the moment. But the win wasn't as satisfying due to how things were with Matthew. Because he wasn't right here at my side, holding my hand, making me laugh or pointing out meaning in art I couldn't understand.

Then the people stepped away, and right behind them was the project. I was able to see the painting for the first time since we'd turned it in. Matted, framed, mounted. It was real.

My heart hammered. I couldn't stop staring. There was Matthew's face, forever linked with mine. Our smiles blended, our eyes sparkling.

He was so handsome.

All the noise around me faded away to the rush of my pulse in my ears. I couldn't tear my gaze away from the painting. How had I not seen it like this before? I guessed the weeks away from the project had given me real clarity. Because right now, I could sense every heart-rending emotion I felt right there on the paper, in every line on his face, every careful attention to detail. Surely everyone else in this room could see it too.

Oh, wow. I loved Matthew.

Heart in my throat, I flicked my attention to his half. He'd done the same attention to detail as I had—granted, in a different way, with more abstract lines and suggestions. But it was there nonetheless. The shell of my ear, the dimple in my chin, the way my mouth crooked in the corner.

We were different, yes, but looking at this painting, I realized it worked. The old and the new, the wild and the calm. They blended together to create a piece that was surprisingly harmonious.

Maybe *we* could work too.

A frustrated cry bubbled in my throat and I bit it back. Why had I walked away from him, from everything he'd offered? Stupid, stupid! I wanted to smack my own forehead. Was it too late?

Could I be brave, like Ava had said, and jump right in, tell him exactly how I felt? Despite my fears?

"Honey, is that him over there?" Mom asked from right behind me. "Is that your art partner, Matthew?"

I spun around and saw Matthew strolling in with his mom and twin sisters close behind. He had on a dark gray suit with an electric blue tie. I drank in the sight of him, my eyes filled with all the love I just now realized I was feeling.

"Mom," I whispered under my breath, "I . . ." I paused. How did I spell out to her how I was feeling, what I needed? Panic bloomed.

"Go talk to him," she said, shoving me forward a touch. "You two can work it out, whatever it is."

I turned to look at her. "You're okay with it? With us?"

She laughed. "Seriously? You've been in a funk for weeks. I want to see you smiling again. Now go, and good luck."

I swigged the last of my punch and dumped the cup in the garbage. My hands were shaking so hard I'd just spill it anyway.

What should I say to him? Words were running through my mind, but I couldn't seem to get them to form a cohesive sentence, much less express the intensity of my emotions.

Matthew's mom was right beside him, whispering in his ear.

He laughed and gave her a quick hug, then moved to the side of the room to look at the artwork. A couple of the judges came over, probably to have the same conversation with him that they'd had with me.

Crud. I couldn't go talk to him right now, not when they were having this talk. I needed a moment to get myself together.

I saw the bathroom sign in the corner and practically ran to it, locking the door behind me. I stared at my reflection in the mirror for a long minute. My makeup looked okay, subtle but there. Lips were glossy pink. Hair was slightly mussed, so I took a moment to smooth it back into place.

Then I turned my back to the mirror and stood there for several more minutes, frozen, scared to death, heart about to thump out of my chest.

He was here. He came.

Stop stalling. But the right words still weren't forming.

Someone knocked on the door. "Occupied?" an older female voice asked.

Time to do this. I straightened my shoulders and willed a large smile to my face as I opened the door. Then I moved past the frail old lady back into the gallery.

The area where he'd been standing before was empty.

Disappointment kicked me in the gut. I scanned the room, but Matthew was nowhere to be found. Where could he have gone? I saw my parents over by the table, talking with his mom and sisters. Everyone else was walking around and eating snacks, drinking punch. Enjoying this moment that had soured so badly for me because of my cowardice.

If I hadn't hidden in the bathroom, I could have pulled him aside, talked to him.

Tears sprang to my eyes. I blinked and moved toward the back door of the gallery, which emptied out into a small patio area for outdoor entertaining. Green plants and vines filled the open space, covering the wrought iron balcony.

I sighed and moved toward the balcony. The city view was gorgeous here—or it would be, if I could see it right now. There were too many tears crowding my eyes. I let the tears streak down my cheeks in hot rivers. Just for a moment, I'd give in to this frustration.

"Corinne," a quiet voice said behind me. A voice I'd know anywhere.

I whipped around. There was Matthew up against the ivy-lined brick wall, staring at me with a frown marring his golden face. His suit jacket was off and draped over his forearm.

I blinked and turned my face away, trying my best to wipe my tears as subtly as possible. I didn't dare speak, not yet. I needed to get my emotions back under control.

"What's wrong?" He stepped toward me.

I opened my mouth to say, *Nothing,* to lie and tell him I was fine. But I couldn't do it. I was tired of telling myself I didn't need him. Tired of acting like art and Matthew and love and all those things I'd never dreamed of before weren't that important to me now.

Because they were. And how they deserved my time and attention too.

"I've been really upset about how things went with us," I finally said.

"Why?" His face was unreadable, back to the emotionless shell I'd last seen. It made it hard for me to open up because I had no idea what he was feeling right now.

"Because . . ." I stared into his eyes and pushed myself to keep going, despite the tremble in my voice. "Because I messed up with you that day you told me you wanted to date me. It was a mistake for me to walk away from it. One I'd give anything to take back."

He didn't move, didn't speak. Just stared.

"You dropped your guard and opened up to me about your feelings. And in response, I threw a bunch of reasons at you about why we wouldn't work, that our worlds were too different to ever intersect. But I was wrong—I think we could work. If we wanted to. Not that I'm saying you want to now, I mean."

Oh wow, the words were pouring out, like the cork had been unplugged from a bottle. I couldn't seem to stop. My cheeks burned in embarrassment, but I kept speaking.

"It took me a while to realize that I'd used school and friends as an excuse to protect myself so I wouldn't get hurt if our relationship fell apart. As a preemptive strike to prevent both of us pain. But then you walked away, and I realized I *was* hurt. That hurt grew as weeks passed and we didn't talk. And I . . ." My throat tightened.

He stepped a fraction closer, those eyes still fixed on me. His Adam's apple bobbed. "You what?" he whispered, his voice gravelly.

I heard the hum of people and cars below, but the city noises faded into a soft lull around us. "I didn't fully realize how I felt about you until I saw our painting today." My face was on fire now, my breath almost ragged as it sawed in and out of my lungs. I felt like I'd run a marathon, winded and overwhelmed and slightly tired.

I was tired of running from myself and my love for him.

"It took me losing you to realize how much I had fallen for you." I closed my eyes, swallowed. There. I'd said it. No taking it back now. "And I've been miserable ever since."

Even if Matthew didn't want me, even if he'd forgotten all about me while we'd been apart, I'd done something I never dreamed I could do. I'd jumped off the cliff without looking for a safety net.

I'd been braver than I'd known I could be.

A soft hand on my chin, a thumb stroking my jaw, had me opening my eyes. Matthew's eyes were hooded, his pupils so dark they almost swallowed up his irises, now a thin blue rim. "Corinne, I've missed you, too," he said.

His other hand wrapped around my lower back, the heat of his palm almost searing me through my thin dress, and he tugged me close. My heart stopped beating for a second, hardly able to accept that Matthew was touching me, that he was looking at me with so much intensity.

"I love you," he continued, and he gave me a crooked grin. "I've loved you for a long time, actually."

"Oh," I said, my voice breathy. "I figured . . . well, I thought . . ."

"I didn't want to push you. You were scared, and I grew frustrated. Then I didn't know how to approach you. But I was going to come find you today. To talk to you one more time and see if . . ." He paused, his head inching close to mine. Lips hovering so, so close. "See if there was a chance."

"There *is* a chance," I said, then shook my head at myself. "Um. Not *just* a chance. I mean—"

"I know what you mean." He chuckled, and the hand on my jaw slid around to cup the back of my neck. His thumb stroked the base of my skull, and small waves of pleasure slid across my skin. "But are you sure you want to do this? I mean, be with me as my girlfriend? Even though we're so very different?" There was a flash of vulnerability in his eyes that made my heart ache.

He was afraid of getting hurt too. Afraid of me giving up on him, on us, when things got tough once school started. Yet he'd laid it all on the line again right now, taking a big risk. Just for me.

I wrapped my arms tightly around him. He smelled like the ocean, and I breathed him in. "We're not that different," I said, pouring every ounce of earnestness into my voice. "We'll make it work out—I have faith. I know we're going to have some hard spots as we figure out how to balance friends and school and art and everything else. But I also know I want to be with you. Unquestionably. I don't want to let you go."

A comfortable silence stretched between us for a minute.

"I . . . I love you, Matthew," I told him. I wanted him to know that he wasn't the only one being vulnerable here. We could support each other.

Matthew's head descended toward mine, blocking out the sun, and his mouth grazed my lips in a soft gesture. I opened my mouth, and he kissed me deeper. We fell into each other, our emotions tangled up and wrapped around us.

I slipped my hands into his thick hair, scarcely able to believe we were finally kissing—it was even better than I'd imagined. Every cell in my body sang from the intensity of us, of this one moment.

Time seemed to still. We finally drew apart, and he pressed a last kiss to my jaw, his breath as ragged as mine.

"You look beautiful today, by the way," he told me as he glanced down at my dress. "That color makes your skin glow."

"You look great too. You should dress like that more often," I teased.

"Kind of hard to sink baskets in a three-piece suit," he deadpanned. His smile widened again. "Ready to go back inside? They're all waiting for us. I, for one, am eager to hear more gushing praise about our artistic eye. And to show off my gorgeous girlfriend to everyone in that room."

I wrapped my hand into the crook of his arm, and we walked

toward the door. A warm breeze ruffled his hair and caressed my bare skin. I cast one last glance at the patio that had made my biggest dream come true—love.

Yes, I'd jumped off the cliff. But so had he. And somehow, we'd caught each other.

"As ready as I'll ever be," I told him, and we went back into the gallery.

Together.

TURN THE PAGE FOR MORE FLIRTY FUN.

fLiRT SUNSET RANCH

A. DESTINY and EMMA CARLSON BERNE

hitched my backpack higher onto my shoulders and brushed back my hair, which already felt ickily greasy. My flight out of Cincinnati had left at six a.m., so I'd skipped a shower. My guitar case seemed to weigh a thousand pounds, and I was beginning to question the wisdom of hauling it all the way out here. As I made my way toward the baggage claim through the cavernous, glass-ceilinged terminal, I tried not to stare as men in actual cowboy hats and boots strode by. Air force soldiers in sleek navy uniforms shouldered big blue duffels. Families with long zippered ski bags struggled past. Out the huge picture windows the mountains hulked, white and blue-gray against an impossibly azure sky. I shivered a little and grinned to myself—this was really Colorado. I was really here, thousands of miles from home, for three months. I wanted to sing my way down the terminal.

I followed the river of people out of the main terminal, stepped onto a down escalator, then followed a long underground passage to an up escalator, then allowed myself to be swept along to another up escalator. I was wondering just how much longer I'd be trailing around this airport when the escalator deposited me in front of several baggage carousels.

I hurried over to the nearest one and scanned the conveyor belt for my khaki-green army surplus duffel. Mom had been so proud when she found it for only five dollars at the thrift store. There it was, riding around and around, looking like an abandoned stuffed animal in the midst of all the black rolling suitcases surrounding it. I elbowed through a scrum of random passengers and reached forward, managing to snag the strap just as the bag moved past. Puffing slightly, I dragged it toward me and let it thump to the floor.

"Hey, thanks for getting my bag," someone said in a southern drawl.

I looked up into the clearest blue eyes I'd ever seen.

A tall boy about my own age was standing beside me. He had a backpack too, and he wore a gray T-shirt that read PACIFIC FOOD CO-OP and frayed khaki shorts with sandals. His black hair fell over his forehead, and his eyes were startlingly light against his tanned skin. He smiled, showing sparkling white teeth. A leather band circled one broad wrist and a narrow silver chain glinted under the collar of his T-shirt.

I closed my mouth, which had fallen open slightly, and cleared my throat. "Ah, sorry. This is my bag." I tried to sound cute and casual, though I think it came out sounding more strained and weird.

He didn't even blink. "It was probably a long flight, huh? You're just a little confused." He flashed me another grin and looped his hand under the strap. "Anyway, like I said, thanks for getting it for me. See you around."

"Hey!" It came out louder than I intended, and several people turned to look. "Excuse me! I don't know who you are, but that's *my* bag. Put it down. Please."

The boy studied the duffel, then looked at me for such a long moment that I flushed, then looked back at the duffel again. A slow grin spread across his face. "Let's see. My bag was my dad's, from the army. So if you're telling the truth, why would you have the same kind of bag? Unless you're in the army yourself." He was teasing me—that much was clear. I wondered if my neck was going all splotchy.

"I'm not in the army. My mom got it at the army surplus store. Okay?" I swiped at the bag, but he slid it back out of my reach and shook his head.

"No way. I can spot a solider a mile away. What's your rank?"

I had to laugh. "I'm not exactly the military type—can't you tell?"

He let his gaze slowly wander from my feet to my head. "No way. You're tough. I mean, look at those muscles." He squeezed my upper arm, and my pulse shot up. "Come on, what do you bench?"

I rolled my eyes. "Very funny. Look, can I please have my bag?"

"Hmm. I say it's mine; you say it's yours. What should we do?" His eyes crinkled up at the edges, and a dimple appeared in his left cheek as his smile deepened. For one electric instant we looked into each other's eyes. Then I cut my gaze away, thoroughly rattled.

"Here." I grabbed the zipper and pulled. The bag fell open, revealing several pairs of purple and pink underwear lying on the top of a mound of jeans and T-shirts. Oops.

The boy laughed out loud, the sound echoing in the big room. "Hey, I can't argue with that. Are those standard military issue?"

My cheeks flamed. Of course I'd forgotten the underwear was on the top. I struggled with the zipper, but a pair of the under-wear was caught in the teeth. Now I had no desire for anything but to get away from this person as fast as I could. "You're funny, I can see that. Hilarious, actually." I yanked at the zipper again.

"It's one of my special talents. Here, let me." The boy pulled hard at the zipper and raked it up to the top.

I exhaled. "Thanks. Anyway. Nice to meet you." A little trickle of sweat ran down my chest, but at least my underwear was safely out of sight again. Without looking at him, I grabbed my bag and marched away toward the glass exit doors.

"Hey, what's your name?" he called after me.

"Private McKinley," I yelled back over my shoulder. Then, just as I turned around again—*bam*. I slammed into the clear glass door.

"Ooh," I moaned, holding my forehead, letting my bag slide from my shoulder. Something dripped from my fingers, and I looked down to see bright blood splotching the floor at my feet.

"Was that on purpose, Private McKinley?" The guy was suddenly beside me, prying my fingers from my numb face. He smelled like peppermint gum. "Because it's cool about the bag and all. You don't have to bleed to make a point."

"I'm fine," I managed, trying to wipe my face but succeeding only in smearing the blood. "Okay? Thanks for your help. This happens to me all the time."

"Nice. Have you ever considered a helmet?" The guy was waving at one of the airport security guards, who came hurrying over.

"Oh now, miss, why don't you come with me to first aid?" The burly man was leaning over me. Then a ticket agent appeared, holding a towel.

"Poor little girl! We have to get you downstairs. . . ."

Another agent strode over. "She might need stitches. . . ."

I pressed the white towel to my brow and looked around. The boy was gone.

First crush · First love · First kiss

fLiRT

LESSONS IN LOVE

A. DESTINY and CATHERINE HAPKA

NEVER TOO LATE

A. DESTINY and RHONDA HELMS

PORTRAIT OF US

A. DESTINY and RHONDA HELMS

SUNSET RANCH

A. DESTINY and EMMA CARLSON BERNE

PUPPY LOVE

A. DESTINY and CATHERINE HAPKA

LOVE IS IN THE AIR

A. DESTINY and ALEX R. KAHLER

SPARKS IN SCOTLAND

A. DESTINY and RHONDA HELMS

OUR SONG

A. DESTINY and ELIZABETH LENHARD

VIRTUALLY IN LOVE

A. DESTINY and CATHERINE HAPKA

LET IT SNOW

A. DESTINY and SUZANNE YOUNG